Welcome to Suite 4B!

Gone to the stables

Jina

Shh!! Studying—
please do not disturb!

Mary Beth

<u>GO AWAY!!!</u>

Andie

Hey, guys!
Meet me downstairs in the
common room. Bring popcorn!

Lauren

Join Andie, Jina, Mary Beth, and Lauren
for more fun at the Riding Academy!

#1 • *A Horse for Mary Beth*
#2 • *Andie Out of Control*
#3 • *Jina Rides to Win*
#4 • *Lessons for Lauren*
#5 • *Mary Beth's Haunted Ride*
#6 • *Andie Shows Off*
#7 • *Jina's Pain-in-the-Neck Pony*
#8 • *The Craziest Horse Show Ever*

And coming soon:

#9 • *Andie's Risky Business*

Magic stopped immediately, then nervously pawed the air. Lauren saw him gather his hind legs under him. He was going to jump!

"Watch out!" Katherine cried as she quickly herded the students out of the way.

The dark horse leaped. He flew through the air, jerking the shank from Dorothy's grasp. He cleared the end of the ramp and slid to a halt on the gravel drive.

Darting forward, Andie grabbed the dangling shank. "Whoa," she commanded.

Lauren breathed a sigh of relief. But as Magic dragged Andie into the barn, her relief turned to anxiety again.

Magic was definitely being a handful today. He and Andie would never win any ribbons. That meant only one thing. She, Lauren, had to ride in the jumper class!

THE CRAZIEST
HORSE SHOW EVER

by Alison Hart

BULLSEYE BOOKS

Random House New York

"Lauren, are bots true worms?" Katherine Parks, Foxhall Academy's dressage instructor, called across the barn's tack room.

Eight girls were scattered around the room, listening attentively. In one corner, a portable heater tried to warm the cold November air that seeped under the door.

Twelve-year-old Lauren Remick wrinkled her nose and shifted nervously on top of the wooden tack box.

Worms? Gross. Why hadn't she gotten a question about cleaning tack or grooming?

"Mmm," Lauren stammered. Her gaze darted to her roommate Mary Beth Finney, who sat next to her. Mary Beth was a beginning rider, so she always studied the questions and answers extra hard.

Mary Beth wiggled her eyebrows under her reddish brown bangs. Lauren tried to remember if that meant yes or no.

"Lauren, we're waiting," Katherine prompted. The young instructor sat on another tack box across the room, the question sheet on her lap. She wore a goosedown vest over a cream-colored turtleneck sweater, and her wavy cropped hair fell softly around her face. "Which is more than the judges are going to do at the show this Saturday," she added with a smile.

"Uh, bots *are* worms?" Lauren guessed.

"Wrong!" Andie Perez, another one of Lauren's roommates, sang out. She was sprawled on the floor under a saddle rack, her riding helmet and winter riding coat draped across her legs. "Bots are the larvae of the botfly. The horse swallows the eggs and the larvae hatch in its stomach."

Katherine nodded. "That's correct, Andie."

Andie scowled at Lauren, her dark eyes flashing. "You need to study, Remick. We want to beat those Manchester geeks."

Lauren flushed. It was true. She hadn't done much studying yet. Usually, Andie wasn't much for studying either, but she was determined that Foxhall's team was going to win this weekend at the interschool horse show—no matter what.

Katherine had told them weeks ago that the teams would be judged on riding ability as well as stable management and general knowledge. *And so far,* Lauren thought gloomily, *I'm flunking the knowledge part.*

Leaning closer to Lauren, Mary Beth whispered, "Wiggling my eyebrows means no, remember?"

Lauren shook her head. That was the problem. She *didn't* remember. Whenever she got nervous, her brain went blank, just the way it did in math class.

Andie, Mary Beth, Lauren, and their fourth roommate, Jina Williams, were all sixth-graders at Foxhall Academy, a private girls' boarding school in Maryland. Every night this week, after study hours were over, they'd quizzed one another on the questions that Katherine had told them would be asked by the judges. Still, Lauren had a hard time remembering the answers. She just couldn't seem to concentrate. Now she forced herself to tune back in to Katherine again.

"There will be ten schools competing at the show," the riding instructor was saying. "We need to be really sharp if we're going to place in the top three."

She glanced at each of the eight girls sitting in the tack room. Besides the four roommates, there was Alicia Sachs and Ginny Cejka, two juniors who competed in dressage; Heidi Olsen, a beginner like Mary Beth; and Missy Miles, an intermediate rider.

"Well, I don't think we have a chance," Andie said, yanking the Scrunchie from her dark ponytail. "None of our best riders will be competing. They're going to be at the A-rated show instead."

"Hey," Jina Williams protested. She was leaning against a saddle rack, her arms crossed. "Are you saying we're lousy riders?"

Lauren was surprised at Jina's sharp tone and snapping gold eyes. Their fourth roommate didn't usually speak out like that.

"Yeah, that's exactly what I'm saying," Andie shot back. "Our team's got a bunch of lame horses and baby riders."

"Your horse isn't exactly a polished performer, Andie," Missy pointed out.

Suddenly, all the girls in the room were arguing.

"We are *not* lousy—"

"So what if—"

"I say we won't—"

"Girls!" Katherine stomped a boot heel on the concrete floor to get their attention.

"Arguing isn't going to get us anywhere," she said when the noise finally died down. "We need to be a *team* this weekend. Besides," she added with a grin, "you're going to be sharing two hotel rooms on Saturday night, so you'd better start getting along."

Mary Beth giggled. "Maybe we can get Missy and Alicia to room with Andie," she whispered to Lauren.

But at least Andie knows all the answers, Lauren thought. If she, Lauren, blew the questions at the show, no one would want to room with her either.

She propped her elbows on her knees and rested her chin in her hands. Okay, maybe she wasn't so hot at answering questions. But she and Whisper, the Foxhall horse she rode, had really clicked this month.

Lauren closed her eyes. She could almost feel Whisper's smooth trot and collected canter. Her last ride had felt perfect. So perfect, they were bound to win a first or second in the dressage test.

"Lauren?"

"Hmmm?" Lauren replied dreamily. A sharp elbow poked her in the side. Startled, she snapped her eyes open. Everybody was staring at her.

"Answer the question, please," Katherine said, frowning. "Describe rhythm in a horse's pace."

Whew. Lauren's shoulders slumped in relief. She could answer that one—she'd just been dreaming about it!

"Rhythm is how even and regular the horse walks, trots, or canters," she said.

Katherine nodded. "Not exactly the answer that's written on the test sheet, but good enough."

"Yay!" Mary Beth slapped Lauren on the shoulder. "I knew you could do it."

Katherine stood up and stretched. "That's enough for today, girls. After dinner, we'll have a major tack-cleaning session." She looked around the room. "Since this is your first overnight this semester, I'm passing out a checklist to remind everyone what they need to bring. Any questions?"

Several girls raised their hands. Lauren

turned to Mary Beth. "Gee, I'm doing better—one question right," she said glumly.

"Oh, don't be so hard on yourself," Mary Beth said, staring at her scuffed paddock boots.

Something in her roommate's voice made Lauren instantly stop thinking about herself. "What's wrong?"

Mary Beth sighed heavily. "Everything." She peered sideways at Lauren. "You don't realize how lucky you are. You're riding gorgeous Whisper in dressage. I'm riding clunky Dangerous Dan in Walk Trot."

"That's not so bad." Lauren tried to sound encouraging.

"And what's even worse," Mary Beth went on, "I don't have any decent riding clothes!"

"What are you two whispering about?" Andie asked, walking over to the tack trunk. She plopped down next to Lauren, shoving her with her hip so hard that Lauren almost knocked Mary Beth off the other side.

"I don't have an outfit for the show," Mary Beth repeated.

"So?" Andie shrugged. "We're going to lose, no matter what."

"No, we aren't," Lauren said, frowning. She was tired of Andie's griping.

"Wanna bet?" Andie retorted. "This is going to be the worst show ever. Can you believe Jina's taking Superstar? She must be nuts."

Lauren glanced up to make sure Jina wasn't listening. Fortunately, Jina was across the room, talking to Alicia.

"Why would she want to take a lame horse to the show?" Andie continued. "Is she *trying* to make us lose?"

"No," Lauren replied. "She's entered Superstar in the Fitting and Showing class. He'll be judged on how good he looks—his grooming, whether his tack's clean, that kind of stuff. I'm sure he'll win."

Andie rolled her eyes. "Oh, sure. That horse hasn't been ridden in ages. He's woolly and fat as a pig. And then Jina's taking that dumb Rotten Apple who bucks her off all the time."

"That's not true." Lauren stuck up for Jina. "First of all, his name is *Applejacks*, not Rotten Apple. And ever since Jina changed saddles, he's been doing just super."

Mary Beth leaned past Lauren. "You know, Perez, you'd better quit cutting everybody

8

down. Especially since you're taking Magic. He just dumped *you*."

"That was two weeks ago," Andie countered. "He's been going great this week. And that means we're going to beat your butt in Walk Trot, Finney. So there." Jumping up from the tack trunk, she flounced across the room.

Mary Beth shook her head. "Andie's such a jerk sometimes," she said to Lauren.

"Well, don't be too hard on her," Lauren said. "I think she's worried about Magic. This will be his first show since his operation."

"She still doesn't have to be so mean," Mary Beth said. "But, she is right about one thing. Foxhall doesn't stand a chance at the show."

Raising her hand, she counted off on her fingers. "Our team has two beginning riders, one lame horse, one half-wild horse, and a pony that bucks. At least you and Whisper are great," she added brightly.

"And you will be too," Lauren said loyally. She leaned back against the wall of the tack room and sighed. "But this is going to be one *crazy* horse show!"

At five-thirty on Saturday morning, Lauren's eyes popped open before her radio alarm even went off. She'd been too excited to sleep. Today was the show!

For a few moments, she lay in her warm bed and stared up at the ceiling. The dorm room was pitch-black. She could hear Mary Beth's soft snores and Andie's mumblings. Jina slept quietly as usual.

Lauren clicked off the alarm. Sitting up, she grabbed her terry bathrobe from the foot of the bed and quickly slipped it on. The room was cold, and she grimaced when her bare feet hit the floor.

"Lauren, is that you?" she heard Mary Beth whisper sleepily.

"It's me." Lauren tiptoed past the wardrobe

to Mary Beth's bed. She could just make out her roommate's shadowy form.

Wrapping her robe tightly around her, Lauren sat down. "Are you excited?" she asked.

Mary Beth nodded. "Really excited," she said in a sleepy voice, "especially since Tommy will be there." Tommy was a boy from the Manchester School whom Mary Beth had met at the Halloween dance.

"Yeah, that'll be cool," Lauren agreed as she stood up. "Well, I'd better get in the bathroom before the others wake up."

She picked up her shower bucket from her dresser and hurried into the bathroom. When she came out twenty minutes later, the light was on. Jina was sitting up in bed, her arms stretched high, yawning. Andie was still huddled under the comforter, her head totally covered.

"So, how do I look?" Mary Beth asked, stepping out from behind the wardrobe door.

Lauren gasped. "You look great!"

Mary Beth beamed. Last night, the roommates had pulled together a riding outfit for her. She was wearing Jina's jodhpurs, Andie's white shirt and wool riding coat, and Lauren's knee straps and stock. The sleeves on the coat were a little short, but her hair was pulled back neatly and her paddock boots gleamed.

"You look like a real equestrienne," Jina said admiringly. She wore a red flannel nightshirt that set off her black hair and chocolate-colored skin. "Boy, I hate getting up this early." She yawned again.

"I was too excited to sleep," Mary Beth said. "This is going to be my first show!"

Jina grinned. "It is pretty exciting." She glanced toward Andie's bed. "And I don't care what Andie says—I think our team is going to do great!"

"Speaking of Andie, who's going to wake up Sleeping Beauty?" Lauren asked. The shape under the covers hadn't moved.

"You mean Sleeping Ugly." Mary Beth giggled.

"I heard that, Finney," Andie's voice came from under the blanket.

Lauren choked back a laugh. She watched as Mary Beth took off her coat and hung it in the garment bag with the other three riding coats. Then her roommate tiptoed over to Andie's bed.

Grabbing the comforter, Mary Beth threw

12

it off Andie. "Wake up, sleepyhead," she sang out.

A groan rose from the curled-up form on the bed. "Get away from me, Finney. I'm never waking up. I don't want to go to the stupid show."

"Oh, quit being so grumpy, Andie," Lauren said. "You want to win more than any of us."

Andie opened one eye. "That's true."

"Well, the only way Foxhall can win is if we convince ourselves that we can beat the other schools. It's not like it's a regular show or anything. There are classes that we can all do well in."

Mary Beth propped herself against Andie's desk so she could take off her paddock boots. "Lauren's right. I mean, I may be a 'baby rider' as Andie says, but I'm still going to try my hardest to win my classes."

"Me too," Jina chimed in. She was pulling a sweatshirt out of her dresser drawer.

Slowly, Andie sat up, her hair a tangled mess. "I guess you guys are right." She smiled apologetically, then yawned. "Sorry I've been such a pain. I've been pretty worried about Magic."

"He'll be fine," Lauren assured her. "And

even if he does get nervous at the show, there's still Ranger. You two should do great in the jumping class."

"We're going to do better than great," Andie said, suddenly leaping out of bed. "We're going to win a blue!"

"That's the spirit," Lauren cheered. She spun around to face Jina and Mary Beth. "Let's do it, roomies! Let's prove that Foxhall is the best!"

"We're here," Dorothy Germaine, Foxhall's stable manager, announced as she slid the door of the minibus open. "Our horses will be stabled in barn A. We're sharing it with Old-fields School."

Lauren jumped from the minibus to the gravel parking lot. For a moment, she gazed in awe at Winter Oaks Horse Center.

The sun was just rising over the Maryland foothills, casting its golden beams on the five barns, huge indoor coliseum, and four outdoor rings. The pastures sparkled with frost, and the barn roofs glowed with reflected light.

"Better shut your mouth, Remick," Andie said, coming up next to her. "You might catch a fly."

"There aren't any flies this time of the year," Mary Beth said. She had unhooked the garment bag from the side of the van and was pulling it out the door.

Jina, Heidi, and Alicia were already around back, helping Dorothy bring out tack, boots, and grooming kits. All the girls wore sweaters and jackets over their jodhpurs or breeches.

"This place is so beautiful," Lauren breathed.

"It *was* beautiful," Andie corrected. Nudging Lauren with her elbow, she pointed to the showground entrance. "Look who's coming to ruin it. Our big competition."

A Manchester School horse van was pulling up the drive. It passed the minibus and stopped at the adjoining barn.

"Oh, wow! Manchester must be in barn B," Mary Beth said excitedly.

Andie rolled her eyes. "Oh, goody. Wimpy Tommy and his friends will be right next to us."

"Hey, are you girls going to help?" Dorothy called. "There's a ton of stuff here. I want to get it all unloaded before our horses arrive."

Lauren hurried to the back of the minibus. Dorothy handed her a bucket full of sponges and sweat scrapers, then threw a stable sheet over her shoulder. The barn manager was an older woman with a no-nonsense style. LOVE ME, LOVE MY HORSE was written across her green sweatshirt.

"What should we do with our suitcases?" Jina asked.

"Leave them here," Dorothy replied. "After we get the horses settled, I'll make a run to the hotel. It's not far."

With the sheet still draped over her shoulder, Lauren followed Mary Beth to the barn. Her roommate kept glancing toward the Manchester van, an expectant look on her face.

"Do you think they're going to unload Tommy from the horse van?" Lauren teased.

Mary Beth blushed under her freckles. "No. I just want to see him, that's all."

"Not me," Andie said, coming up beside them. Her arms were loaded down with boots zipped up in brightly colored boot bags. "He'll probably be competing against me in the jumping class. And he's not a bad rider."

"I'm glad *I'm* not jumping," Lauren said. After last summer's clinic, jumping was definitely not her favorite thing. The whole idea of leaving the ground scared her to death.

When the girls stepped through barn A's sliding door, Lauren stopped to look around. Twelve stalls ran down each side of a wide concrete aisle. Each school would have half a barn. Barn A was the smallest barn at Winter Oaks, but since Foxhall was bringing only ten horses, the girls would have two extra stalls for storing feed and equipment.

"Put the buckets and stuff in a spare stall," Dorothy said as she came into the barn. Heidi and Jina followed behind her, carrying a hay bale between them.

"You'll have the whole morning to organize the equipment," Dorothy added before turning to leave. "The judges will do today's barn check during the lunch break."

Lauren grimaced. That didn't give them much time, especially since they still had to braid and groom.

She glanced at the others. They were all staring at the growing pile of stuff. Mary Beth and Heidi looked overwhelmed. Since this was their first show, Lauren could understand why.

"Don't worry, we'll get everything done," Lauren assured them.

"The horses are here!" Jina called suddenly, pointing out the half-open door.

With squeals of excitement, the six girls raced from the barn. Dorothy was standing in the drive, waving to the driver of the large Fox-hall van. Behind the van, Katherine drove a pickup truck with a trailer. Ginny, Missy, and a stack of buckets were squashed in the front seat next to her.

Andie and Lauren ran to the pickup. Ranger, the school horse Andie rode, and Whisper were riding in the trailer.

When Katherine climbed from the truck, Lauren saw that her face was pale. "What's wrong?" she asked.

Katherine frowned. "Ranger stomped and kicked the whole ride."

"Is he okay?" Andie asked anxiously. Without waiting for an answer, she swung open the trailer's front door and stuck her head inside.

Ranger's neck was dark with sweat. He nickered and pawed the rubber mat. Lauren could just see Whisper's nose and ears on the other side of the hay net. She hoped the mare was all right.

"Let's unload him," Katherine said grimly as she unlatched the trailer ramp.

Andie hooked the lead rope onto Ranger's halter and unsnapped him from the quick-release trailer tie. "Ready!" she called back.

Lauren ran around to help Katherine. When they lowered the heavy tailgate to the ground, Lauren gasped in horror. It was splashed with blood!

"Looks like he cut his hock," Katherine said. "Easy, buddy," she crooned. She put one hand reassuringly on Ranger's rump, then unsnapped the tail bar.

"Back him out slowly," she told Andie.

Lauren's eyes widened as Ranger backed cautiously onto the ramp. Bright blood covered his right hock and dotted his shipping boots.

Katherine shook her head. "I knew we should have put him in the van."

"Will he be okay?" Andie asked again worriedly.

"It's hard to tell," Katherine said. "Go find Dorothy. Tell her we need to hose his leg off."

Hands on her hips, the riding instructor studied Ranger as Andie led him toward the barn. As he walked, he jerked his right hind leg high as if it hurt him.

"Well, one thing's for sure," Katherine said with a sigh. "Ranger won't be showing today."

She turned and looked at Lauren. "That means you'll have to enter a jumping class."

Lauren's jaw dropped. *A jumping class!*

No! she thought frantically. She couldn't enter a jumping class. She would ruin the whole show. She'd just have to tell Katherine she wasn't going to jump—not in a million years!

"But, Katherine, I can't enter a jumping class," Lauren protested shrilly.

Katherine handed her a lead rope. "You have to, Lauren. You and Whisper are the only pair that has experience over fences. And if we don't have two team members jumping, we'll automatically lose points."

"B-but," Lauren stammered. Her heart was pounding so hard, she could hardly talk.

Katherine stared at her strangely. "You jumped Whisper at the clinic this summer, right? I remember the two of you looked good together."

Lauren gulped. "Well, yes, we jumped a little. But we haven't jumped since then."

"Don't worry," Katherine said, patting her on the shoulder. "I'll enter you in Beginners

Over Fences. You'll practically be able to step over the jumps. Now let's hurry and get Whisper unloaded. We have a lot to do!"

Katherine started around to the back of the trailer. Panicking, Lauren ran after her. She caught the instructor's arm. "Why can't Andie or Jina ride Whisper in a jumping class?"

Katherine frowned. "You know the rules, Lauren. Competitors can switch classes, but not horses." She smiled reassuringly. "Hey, don't worry. You'll do fine. Now go unhook Whisper so we can unload her."

For a split second, Lauren stood frozen, staring at Katherine. How could she make the instructor understand?

It was bad enough that she wouldn't do such a hot job on the knowledge test. But if Katherine made her jump, she'd blow the whole show—big time.

Just then Dorothy bustled up. "Ranger's okay," she told Katherine. "It's a minor gash. Just made a lot of blood. Andie's hosing the leg down."

Lauren exhaled with relief. *Thank goodness.*

"But he's definitely off." Dorothy shook her head. "No showing today."

Lauren's heart clunked to her toes.

"That leaves only Missy jumping T.L.," Dorothy continued. "We're going to lose points right off the bat."

"No, we won't," Katherine said. "Whisper and Lauren can jump. Lauren just needs a little schooling to build up her confidence. Right, Lauren?"

Lauren smiled weakly.

"Miss Katherine! Miss Dorothy!" someone hollered.

The two women turned. Pete Previtti, who was often hired to van the Foxhall horses, was waving to them.

Dorothy handed Katherine a lead shank. "Come on. We need to get those other horses unloaded. Pete needs to get back to Foxhall to transport two more horses to that other show."

"This day sure did get complicated fast," Katherine grumbled before jogging after Dorothy. "Lauren, keep an eye on Whisper," she called over her shoulder.

"Okay," Lauren called back. With a heavy heart, she turned and walked to the front of the trailer. Katherine was right. Things sure had gotten complicated.

When she opened the other side door, Whisper greeted her with a throaty nicker.

Lauren ruffled the mare's soft forelock.

"Sorry you're still in here, girl. We didn't forget about you. I wish I could forget about this stupid show, though."

Tears pricked Lauren's eyes. She felt trapped. If she *didn't* enter the jumping class, she'd let her team down. But if she *did* enter, she'd probably blow the class. Because she really didn't want to jump—not after last summer.

Lauren sighed. She might as well face it. No matter what she did, she'd be a loser.

Just then, a sudden loud bellow startled Lauren. Whisper stuck her head through the trailer door and whinnied a reply. Lauren stepped away from the trailer so she could see what was happening.

The side door to the van was open and the ramp had been lowered. Dorothy stood at the top of the ramp holding Magic. A chain lead shank was over his nose.

Head raised high, Magic looked around excitedly with white-rimmed eyes. Lauren thought the dark brown gelding was gorgeous. Gorgeous, but definitely hard to handle.

When Magic was younger, he'd had a bad accident in a trailer. This past week Dorothy and Andie had worked hard loading him and unloading him, trying to get him used to it again. But Magic's lathered neck and flicking ears told Lauren he was still nervous.

With another bellow, the big Thoroughbred began to pull Dorothy down the ramp. Andie, Jina, Missy, and Katherine stood at the bottom. Andie was anxiously biting her lip.

"Whoa," Dorothy barked. She tugged hard on the chain, trying to slow him down.

Magic stopped immediately, then nervously pawed the air. Lauren saw him gather his hind legs under him. He was going to jump!

"Watch out!" Katherine cried as she quickly herded the students out of the way.

The dark horse leaped. He flew through the air, jerking the shank from Dorothy's grasp. He cleared the end of the ramp and slid to a halt on the gravel drive.

Darting forward, Andie grabbed the dangling shank. "Whoa," she commanded.

Magic swung sideways, then butted her with his nose as if he was happy to see her. Lauren breathed a sigh of relief.

But as Magic dragged Andie into the barn, her relief turned to anxiety again.

Since Andie couldn't show Ranger, that just

left Magic. And he was definitely being a handful today. She doubted he and Andie would win any ribbons—even in an easy Walk Trot class.

That meant only one thing. She, Lauren, *had* to ride in the jumper class. Her team would really need the points.

All she had to do was convince herself she could do it.

"Lauren? Are you in there?" Mary Beth called into Whisper's stall later that morning.

"Yup," Lauren replied. She was standing on an overturned bucket, finishing Whisper's last braid.

Mary Beth pushed open the stall door.

Lauren peered over Whisper's neck. Her roommate was gingerly patting the mare's nose. Her expression seemed worried.

"What's wrong?" Lauren asked.

"Nothing."

Lauren doubled the last braid under and knotted the brown thread. "Yes, there is. I can tell."

Mary Beth sighed. "You're right. There *is* something wrong. But it's too silly to talk about."

"No, it's not." Lauren inspected her braiding job, then jumped off the bucket. She ducked under Whisper's neck. "There isn't anything wrong with Dan, is there? We don't need a third disaster."

Mary Beth looked puzzled. "A third disaster?"

Me in a jumping class, Lauren answered silently. *That will be the biggest disaster of them all.*

She dropped her braiding supplies in her grooming box. Should she confide in Mary Beth? Her roommate was probably the only one who would understand how worried she was.

"Oh, you must mean Magic," Mary Beth went on. "He *is* a disaster. Andie's hand-walking him in one of the turnout paddocks. She's pretty upset. If he doesn't calm down, she may not have a horse to show."

"That would be awful," Lauren said.

"And you should see Manchester's setup," Mary Beth rushed on. "It's disgusting—all their stuff matches! The horse blankets and tack trunks are green and white, and they have a huge banner with the school's name on it draped across the aisle."

"Oh, great." Lauren sighed. No, she definitely shouldn't tell Mary Beth about her jumping problem. She wouldn't tell *anybody*, she decided. The Foxhall team was having enough troubles.

She glanced sideways at Mary Beth. "You still haven't told me what you're so worried about."

Her roommate flushed. "Well, you know how excited I was about seeing Tommy. I thought he'd be just as excited to see me. But when I went over to Manchester's barn, he barely said hello. He had to school some horse over a bunch of fences."

Tommy. Fences. Lauren felt a sudden surge of hope.

Last Halloween weekend, when Manchester had visited Foxhall, students from both riding programs had competed in games. Lauren remembered how Tommy had steered Lukas effortlessly over a bunch of obstacles. He was one of the best riders she'd ever seen.

If anyone could help her do well in the jumping class, it was Tommy. *If* he didn't mind giving a hand to the competition, of course. But she had a feeling he'd do it. He seemed like a real nice guy.

"Lauren?" Mary Beth interrupted her thoughts. "You didn't even hear what I said."

Lauren grinned slowly. "No, I heard."

Mary Beth raised her brows. "Then why are you smiling like that?"

Lauren's grin widened. "I just may have figured out a way to prevent a third disaster!" she said.

4

"The barn looks great!" Lauren said enthusiastically an hour later. She twirled slowly in the aisle, checking out the team's handiwork.

The eight girls had spent the rest of the morning arranging the feed and buckets in one stall and the tack and grooming supplies in the other. Clothes and boots had been stashed in the minibus. The aisle had been raked clean and the stalls bedded with fresh straw.

"I think it looks pretty good, too," Missy Miles said. The older girl was already dressed in her hunt coat and breeches. She was entered in the second class, Jumper Warm-up. "We worked hard and it shows."

"It looks okay," Mary Beth grumbled. Dirt streaked her freckled nose, and hay clung to her jeans. "But none of our equipment matches like—"

Andie clapped a hand over Mary Beth's mouth. "If I hear one more thing about Manchester's stupid color-coordinated tack trunks, I'm going to puke," she said. "Besides, their horses don't look as good as ours." She nodded toward Superstar, who was standing quietly next to Jina.

Jina beamed proudly. She had polished her horse's hooves and slicked him with a soft towel until he shone. Lauren was sure he'd win a ribbon in his Fitting and Showing class.

Mary Beth pried Andie's hand from her mouth. "You don't have to suffocate me."

"So how's Magic doing?" Missy asked Andie.

Andie grinned. "After I longed him for twenty minutes, he finally settled down. I think he'll do okay."

"I guess that leaves just me with a bad case of nerves," Mary Beth said in a low voice to Lauren as she chewed a fingernail. "Dan and I are in the fourth class, Beginners Walk Trot."

Lauren squeezed her friend's wrist. She wished she could tell Mary Beth that she wasn't the only one who was worried about her classes.

"Well, this is it, guys," Alicia said. "We all better get ready. But first we need a cheer for good luck."

The eight girls huddled in a circle, their arms around each others' shoulders. "Foxhall, Foxhall, we can do it *all!*"

At the end of the chant, the girls raised their arms and slapped palms.

We'll need all the luck we can get, Lauren thought. She glanced at her watch. Tommy was entered in the Jumper Warm-up, too. If she could just sneak out . . .

"Lauren, can you help me?" Mary Beth asked. "I'm not sure how to get my hair in this thing." She held up a brown hairnet.

Alicia plucked the net from Mary Beth's fingers. "I'll give you a hand," she said with a laugh. "Come over here. I've got a mirror."

Lauren turned to go. If she hurried, she could probably catch Tommy in the practice ring.

"Lauren!" Jina waved from the doorway of Superstar's stall. "Can you saddle Superstar while I put on my boots?"

Lauren hesitated. She'd rather talk to

Tommy, but if her teammates needed her . . .

"Sure." With a sigh, she jogged to the stall and took Superstar's reins. "I'll take him down to the ring after I saddle him. We'll wait for you there."

Jina nodded, and Lauren set the saddle on the handsome gray, making sure the snow-white pad was even all around before tightening the girth. She pulled a clean towel from Jina's grooming box and slung it over her shoulder. Then she led Superstar out the barn door.

A warm November sun peeked through the clouds. The show grounds bustled with riders getting ready for their first classes. Lauren felt a tingle of excitement. But as she watched a girl school a pony over a practice jump, the tingle disappeared and a hard knot formed in her stomach.

Every time she watched someone jump, she remembered the accident she'd seen at the Foxhall riding clinic last summer. The horse galloping into the fence, hitting it hard. The rider flying helplessly through the air.

"Hey, Lauren!" Missy waved from the practice arena. She was mounted on T.L., which was short for Too Lazy to Race. An ex-race-horse, T.L. had found his calling as a Foxhall school horse.

"Hi, Missy." Lauren led Superstar closer to the fence. She craned her neck, trying to find Tommy.

Missy trotted T.L. over, halting him in front of Lauren and Superstar. The two horses touched noses, and Superstar squealed.

"I hear we're going to be the only two jumping from Foxhall," Missy said. She wore a dark blue coat over buff-colored breeches.

Lauren grimaced. "No, *you'll* be jumping. I'll be holding on to Whisper's mane, hoping I can get around the course without falling off. I'm lucky Katherine only entered me in Beginners Over Fences."

"But I thought Whisper was a good jumper," Missy said, sounding puzzled.

"*She* is," Lauren replied. "I'm not." Then she spotted Tommy leaping a large-boned bay over what seemed to her to be a gigantic fence. But horse and rider sailed over as if it wasn't even there.

"I'm afraid T.L. and I don't have a chance against those two," Missy said gloomily.

"That's Tommy Isaacson. You know, as in Ralph Isaacson."

Missy's brows shot up. "You mean Ralph Isaacson, the Grand Prix rider? That guy is his son?"

Lauren nodded. "Yep."

Missy whistled. "Well, now I won't feel so bad if he beats me and T.L." She gathered her reins. "I guess I'd better take a practice jump. I have to make sure Too Lazy isn't too lazy."

Lauren wished her teammate good luck. Still holding Superstar, she leaned on the top rail, trying to catch Tommy's eye. If only he'd come over to say hello. Then she could ask him about helping her this afternoon.

"Lauren!" someone called sharply.

She spun around. Jina was jogging toward her across the gravel drive, her dark cheeks flushed from the cold air.

"I've been looking everywhere for you," she called. "Hurry, or we'll be late!" She gestured for Lauren to follow her to another outdoor ring. Already, riders were leading their horses through the in gate.

"Oh, Jina, I'm so sorry," Lauren apologized. Clucking to Superstar, she trotted him to the ring.

Jina looked annoyed as she jerked the clean

towel from Lauren's shoulder. She had just enough time to wipe Superstar's nostrils and hooves before leading him into the ring.

Lauren smacked herself on the side of the head. "Stupid," she mumbled. She should have had Superstar ready and waiting. Instead, she'd been worrying about herself.

"Do you want me to hit you, too?" Andie asked sweetly as she hobbled up to the ring-side.

"No thanks." Lauren frowned as she looked down at Andie's leg. "What's wrong with you? Is your knee bothering you again?"

"Yeah. Leading Magic did me in. It's a good thing I'm not jumping Ranger today."

Good for you, maybe, Lauren thought. "Are you going to be okay?" she asked aloud.

"Sure." Andie directed her attention to the class. "So how's the piggy horse doing?"

"Superstar's not fat," Lauren protested. She studied the twenty entrants lined up in the center of the ring. A judge wearing a tweed golfing cap, leather sportcoat, and corduroys walked slowly around the horses. Clipboard in hand, he inspected each one from head to hoof.

Andie snorted. "Yes, he is. He's still the best-looking horse out there, though. And Jina's got him really slicked up. That's one blue ribbon for our team," she added confidently.

"Don't count any ribbons before they're won," Lauren cautioned.

"Hey, Ms. Pessimistic," Andie retorted, "weren't you the one who said we could beat those other schools?"

"Yeah," Lauren muttered. *But that was before I knew I had to jump.*

She crossed her fingers when the judge came to Superstar. Head high, ears pricked alertly, the Thoroughbred posed as if he were on stage. The judge studied him for a moment, then nodded slightly and scribbled something on his clipboard.

Andie poked Lauren. "The judge likes him," she whispered excitedly. "It's a good thing someone wearing a goofy cap like that can tell a quality horse."

Lauren bit back a giggle. "Shhh. He might hear you."

When the judge stopped in front of Superstar to check his bridle, Lauren gave Jina the thumbs-up sign. Jina flashed her a quick smile, then gazed ahead with a serious expression as the judge continued to write.

Suddenly, Superstar reached up and snatched the judge's cap right off his bald head. Startled, the man stumbled backward. Jina gasped and lunged for the hat, but she was too late.

Holding the brim between his teeth, Superstar flapped the cap in the air. He looked so comical that Lauren had to laugh. Beside her, Andie burst into hysterical guffaws.

The judge's face turned bright red. Scowling, he reached up and jerked the cap from Superstar's mouth, ripping the brim.

"Oh, I'm so sorry!" Lauren heard Jina say. "He's never done that before!"

Still scowling, the judge slapped the torn cap back on his head. Superstar lifted his lip, showing his teeth. And when people on the fence rail started laughing even harder, he danced in place, his tail held high.

Stepping clear of Superstar, the judge crossed out what he'd written on the clipboard. At the same time, he muttered something to Jina.

Jina pressed her lips together. Eyes downcast, she nodded slowly as she listened.

Lauren groaned. She could tell from Jina's

expression that the judge had given her bad news.

That means bad news for Foxhall, Lauren thought gloomily. *And one more disaster our team doesn't need!*

5

"I knew it," Andie grumbled as she leaned on the fence rail beside Lauren. "I knew Jina shouldn't have brought that horse."

"Oh, lighten up, Andie," Lauren said. Suddenly she felt determined not to let all the disasters get to her. "You're as bad as that sour-faced judge. I mean, you have to admit, it *was* funny."

Andie chuckled. "True. Too bad the judge doesn't have a sense of humor."

A few minutes later, the winners were announced. "And sixth place goes to Superstar, owned by Jina Williams," the announcer finally blasted over the loudspeaker.

Lauren let out her breath. At least Jina had won *something*. But the big frown on Jina's face told Lauren her roommate wasn't very happy with a green ribbon.

"Congratulations!" Lauren said cheerfully as Jina led Superstar from the ring.

Jina shot her roommate a stormy look. "We would have *won* until the circus horse here decided to perform his amazing trick."

"Look on the bright side," Andie said, taking the reins from Jina. "Everyone got a big laugh out of it."

Jina raised her brows in surprise. "Aren't you guys mad we didn't win?"

Lauren shook her head. "Of course not."

"Hey, maybe you can make Foxhall famous by going on that TV program that has those stupid pet tricks," Andie said.

Jina started to laugh. Lauren was glad her roommate felt better.

"So, Jina, what did the judge say to you after Superstar grabbed his cap?" Lauren asked.

Jina giggled hysterically. "He said, 'Young lady, that hat cost me fifty dollars!'"

Andie and Lauren looked at each other and burst out laughing, too.

Just then, Mary Beth came up. "What is *wrong* with you guys? I mean, get serious. I

41

need *help*. Has anyone seen Dorothy?"

Lauren wiped the tears of laughter from her cheeks. She knew Mary Beth was super-nervous. "No, we haven't seen her. What do you need help with?"

"Everything!" Mary Beth wailed. "My class is in twenty minutes and I haven't even tacked Dan up yet."

Lauren looped her arm through Mary Beth's. "Come on," she said, turning her toward the barn. "I'll help you."

Mary Beth nodded. Her freckled cheeks were pale.

"Hey, I saw Tommy a little while ago," Lauren said, hoping to cheer her friend up. "He asked about you."

"He did?" Mary Beth stopped in her tracks, her face brightening.

Immediately, Lauren regretted her fib. Why had she said such a dumb thing?

"Well, yeah. Only he was getting ready for his class, so we didn't talk long."

A smile formed slowly on Mary Beth's lips. "Wow. He asked about me," she repeated dreamily, following Lauren into the barn.

"Why don't you get your bridle?" Lauren said. "I'll check Dan."

On her way to Dan's stall, Lauren looked in on Whisper. The pretty chestnut mare was contentedly munching hay, her braids still neat. Stabled next to her was Applejacks, the light-gray pony that Jina was riding later in the day. As Lauren passed by, he stuck his head over the wooden stall door.

"Hey, cutie pie." Lauren scratched his forehead. She wondered if Whitney Chambers, Applejacks's young owner, was going to come to watch his first show.

Dan's grooming box was outside his stall. Lauren picked it up and unlatched the door. Dan was dozing in a corner, his lower lip hanging, one back leg cocked. He looked like a big Saint Bernard.

"Wake up," she told him. He swiveled one ear toward her. She was glad to see that Mary Beth had groomed the huge horse until his chestnut coat gleamed. Still, she wiped him down with a clean towel, then added a little hoof polish on a few spots her friend had missed.

"Here's my stuff!" Mary Beth said breathlessly as she bustled into the stall. "Sorry I took so long. I couldn't figure out which bridle was his. They all look alike."

Lauren took the bridle and held it up. "Are you sure this is Dan's? It looks small."

"Katherine thought it was."

"Did you ask Dorothy?"

Mary Beth shook her head. She was hopping nervously from foot to foot. "Dorothy left. She had to go help Mrs. Caufield at that other show. She won't be back until tonight," she added, her voice rising.

Uh-oh, Lauren thought. That left the team with Katherine. The dressage instructor was an excellent rider, but it was no secret that it was Dorothy who kept the barn running smoothly.

"That's okay," Lauren said aloud. "We'll get Dan ready."

But even after she'd lengthened the cheek pieces, the bridle was still too small.

"You'll have to get another one," Lauren said, starting to feel frustrated. "No, wait. *I'll* get it. You saddle Dan."

Mary Beth nodded. "We've got to hurry." She tapped her watch face. "It's getting late."

"Okay." Lauren jogged down the aisle and into the spare stall. She grabbed the first bridle that looked giant-size. When she came back, Mary Beth was standing outside the stall, biting her nails.

"What's wrong now?" Lauren asked.

"I can't get the girth to fit!"

Lauren rolled her eyes. *What next?*

"Then we'll just have to get a bigger one," she said, trying to keep calm. She took a deep breath and stepped into the stall. But when she looked at Dan, she started giggling.

"No wonder the girth doesn't fit! You put the saddle on backward!"

"What?" Mary Beth spun around. Her mouth dropped open. The saddle was perched awkwardly on Dan's wide back, the pommel facing his tail.

"I can't believe I did that!" Mary Beth groaned. "I've just been so nervous."

"Everyone makes mistakes," Lauren said. "Come on, let's fix it up."

Working together, the girls got Dan saddled and bridled. When the three of them finally emerged from the barn, the announcer was calling for all riders in Beginners Walk Trot to enter the ring. Lauren was amazed at how many horses were crowding toward the in gate.

She gave Mary Beth a leg up and handed her the crop. Her friend looked grim.

"Just pretend this is a lesson," Lauren

45

advised. "And have fun!" she called as Mary Beth steered Dan through the gate.

For a few minutes, Lauren watched the beginners guide their horses around the ring. Then she began to chew her lip worriedly.

She *had* to talk to Tommy—soon.

She glanced over her shoulder. The Jumper Warm-up was still going on in the other ring. Missy and T.L. were hanging around outside the in gate. At first, she didn't see Tommy, but then she glimpsed him trotting the big bay at one end of the ring.

Tommy must be jumping next! she thought excitedly. She glanced back at Mary Beth. Her friend was sitting stiffly in the saddle, her lips pressed in a straight line. Dan ambled along quietly.

They'll be fine, Lauren told herself as she took off for the jumping ring.

When she reached the other ring, Tommy was coming down the last line of fences. Smooth as silk, he and the big horse leaped over an in and out and then a gate, clearing them by a mile. The crowd clapped when Tommy finally slowed the horse to a jog.

Lauren eagerly turned toward the exit gate, then froze. A bunch of Manchester guys with green and white crests on the front of their hunt coats were rushing up to congratulate Tommy.

Lauren suddenly realized how stupid her idea had been. Tommy wasn't going to help her. He rode for a rival team. Besides, she didn't even know him that well.

Whirling around, she started to hurry away.

"Hey, Lauren!" Tommy had halted his horse a few feet away. He grinned and waved to her.

Lauren stopped in her tracks. The crowd of guys around Tommy had disappeared. "Oh, hi, Tommy," she said, feeling awkward. "That was a great ride."

"Thanks." He slid off the bay. "But it wasn't me. Gemstone here is pretty green, but he's a terrific jumper."

As he pulled the reins over the horse's head, Lauren stepped closer and patted the horse's sweaty neck. "And you're a terrific rider," she said, smiling at Tommy.

"So how's Foxhall doing so far?" he asked as he ran up a stirrup. His green eyes twinkled mischievously. Lauren could see why Mary Beth liked him.

"We're all doing great," Lauren fibbed.

"Except me. Uh, I have a little problem."

"Yeah?" He loosened the girth.

Lauren nodded. "Yeah. A problem I could use some help with," she said slowly, eyeing him to see how he'd react.

Tommy raised one brow. "So what is it? Maybe I can help," he said, sounding sincere.

Lauren pressed her nails into her palms, not sure what to do. What if she confided in Tommy and he laughed at her? What if he said no?

"Well, I'm entered in a jumping class," Lauren finally blurted. "Only I haven't jumped since this summer and I was wondering if you could help me. I know you're from the competition, but I don't want to ask anyone from Foxhall because so many things have happened and I don't want them to know how nervous I am—but really you can say no—"

"Lauren," Tommy interrupted.

Gulping, she looked over at him. "Yes?"

"I'll help you."

"You will?" she asked in surprise.

"Sure." He grinned.

Lauren grinned back, feeling a huge weight lift off her shoulders. Everything was going to be okay!

"Will you give me a hand putting this cooler on Gemstone?" Tommy asked, but Lauren barely heard him. *He was going to help her jump!*

And if everything worked out right, no one from Foxhall would know. They'd never find out she was scared to jump, and they wouldn't know a rival team member had helped her.

"Lauren, can you please pull the cooler down?" Tommy said, louder this time.

"Hmmm?" Lauren snapped back to attention. Tommy had ducked under Gemstone's neck. A blanket was draped across the horse's withers.

Tommy peered over the horse's broad back. "Pull the cooler down on your side," he repeated patiently.

"Oh, right! Sorry." Lauren grabbed the green and white wool cloth.

Manchester's colors, she thought. The school crest was even on the side of the blanket. Mary Beth had been right. Manchester was definitely prepared for the show.

"Do you think you'll win a ribbon?" she asked Tommy as she smoothed the cooler over Gemstone's rear.

He shrugged as he fastened the surcingle. "Who knows? We jumped clean, but Gemstone's time was slow. I'm more interested in a good ride than a ribbon."

Suddenly, Lauren remembered Mary Beth. "Mary Beth's riding in Beginners Walk Trot," she said. "We should go cheer her on."

"I can for a minute," Tommy replied, his eyes still on the surcingle, "but I've got to keep Gemstone walking."

Lauren led the way to the ring. Mary Beth and Dan were just trotting past. Mary Beth stared straight ahead and her lips were scrunched in a determined line. Heidi Olsen, the other Foxhall beginner, looked much more relaxed as she trotted behind on Windsor.

"Mary Beth doesn't look like she's having a

lot of fun," Tommy said after they'd watched for a few minutes.

"She's too nervous to have fun." Lauren giggled. "Right before her class, she put the saddle on backward!"

"Backward?" Tommy repeated in disbelief. Lauren nodded and the two of them started laughing. Just then, Mary Beth and Dan jogged past again. Her eyes darted to Lauren and Tommy before she jerked her gaze forward again.

"Well, I'd better keep Gem moving," Tommy said finally. "When do you want to practice?"

"How about after lunch?" Lauren suggested. "I have a dressage test at three. I don't jump until tomorrow, but I'd like to school today."

"That's fine." Tommy turned Gemstone around. "We can meet at the practice ring."

"The practice ring?" Lauren hesitated, picturing everyone in the world watching. "Uh, is there somewhere a little more private?"

Tommy thought for a moment. "How about the indoor ring in the coliseum? A few kids were schooling in there."

"Great." Lauren nodded. "Thanks, Tommy."

"No problem." He touched the rim of his helmet. "And say hi to Mary Beth for me."

Lauren waved good-bye, then turned back to watch her roommate. The horses were lined up in the center of the ring now. As the judge walked down the line, he asked each one to back up. When it was Dan's turn, the big horse stepped back two strides and halted. Mary Beth patted him, looking relieved.

Finally, the judge handed his sheet to the ringmaster. Lauren held her breath. *Please let Mary Beth get a ribbon*, she prayed silently. She knew how much it would mean to her friend.

"First place goes to Windsor, owned by Foxhall Academy and ridden by Heidi Olsen."

"Yay!" Lauren hollered. A blue for Foxhall!

On the other side of the ring, a huge cheer went up. Lauren recognized Jina, Andie, and the rest of the Foxhall team. She ran over to join them.

"Isn't that great?" Jina exclaimed when Lauren came up. "Our first blue!"

"How do you think Mary Beth did?" Lauren asked.

Andie looked around Jina. "She looked great—for a stiff."

"Oh, come on. Mary Beth wasn't that bad," Lauren protested.

"And fifth place goes to Dangerous Dan, owned by Foxhall Academy and ridden by Mary Beth Finney," the announcer reported a minute later.

Mary Beth's mouth dropped open. She looked totally shocked.

"Way to go, Finney!" Andie hollered.

"Yay, Mary Beth!" Lauren and Jina chorused. And as Mary Beth walked Dan toward the ringmaster to get pinned, the members of the team shouted, "Foxhall, Foxhall, we can do it all!"

"Let's go congratulate her," Lauren said to Jina and Andie.

The three of them ran to the exit gate. Dan walked proudly from the ring, the pink ribbon fluttering from his brow band. Mary Beth's mouth was still hanging open.

"I don't believe it," she muttered when Lauren, Andie, and Jina came up to her.

"I don't either," Andie teased.

Lauren patted Mary Beth's boot. "Congratulations!"

Ignoring her, Mary Beth dismounted. "Do you really think Dan and I did that well?" she asked Jina and Andie.

Jina patted Dan heartily. "Definitely. Fifth out of fifteen riders is great."

"And unless you paid him off, the judge wouldn't have pinned you if he thought you stunk," Andie added.

"Thanks," Mary Beth said.

"No, really." Lauren nodded seriously. "You were terrific." Mary Beth didn't even look at her.

"Hey, teammate, we did it!" Heidi Olsen came up, leading Windsor. Alicia and Ginny were with her. Heidi and Mary Beth slapped palms.

Just then the announcer called, "And the results of class two, Jumper Warm-up—"

"Let's go see if Missy pinned," Andie said excitedly.

The seven girls and two horses hurried over to the other ring just in time to see Tommy jog Gemstone toward the ringmaster, who held out a blue ribbon.

"Oh, rats, Tommy got first place," Andie grumbled.

Lauren nudged Mary Beth. "I think it's

54

neat," she whispered so the others wouldn't hear.

Mary Beth ignored her and stared straight ahead.

Lauren frowned, totally puzzled. *What is going on?* she wondered.

"Fourth place goes to T.L., owned by Foxhall Academy and ridden by Missy Miles," the announcer blasted.

"Way to go, Missy!" Andie, Alicia, Jina, and Heidi whooped.

Lauren leaned closer to Mary Beth. "Are you all right?" she asked in a low voice.

"I'm fine," Mary Beth snapped.

Surprised, Lauren jerked back. She'd never seen Mary Beth act like this.

Abruptly, Mary Beth spun around and led Dan from the rail. Lauren hesitated for a second, then ran after her. She had to find out what was going on.

"Hey." Lauren fell into step beside Mary Beth. "What's wrong with you?"

Mary Beth stopped dead in her tracks. Whirling around, she faced Lauren, her expression stony. "You and Tommy. That's what's wrong with me."

Lauren's brows shot up. "Me and Tommy!"

she sputtered, really confused now. "What about me and Tommy?"

"The two of you, laughing when I rode past." Sticking her face in Lauren's, Mary Beth narrowed her eyes. "So what were you laughing about? How *dumb* I looked?"

"No!" Lauren protested. "I was telling Tommy how you were so nervous you saddled Dan backward."

"Oh, *thanks*, pal," Mary Beth said, her tone sarcastic. "Now he knows I'm a total riding klutz, thanks to you. Come on, Dan," she said. Impatiently tugging on the reins, she strode toward the barn.

"But, Mary Beth!" Lauren called, jogging to catch up with her roommate again. "Tommy thought putting on the saddle backward was funny. We didn't think *you* were funny."

"Sure," Mary Beth retorted. She stormed into the barn.

Lauren followed her, still trying to explain. "We weren't—" Suddenly, she stopped, staring down the aisle in shock.

Loose hay was strewn everywhere. Several grooming kits had been dumped over, two blankets lay wadded against the wall, and horse manure dotted the concrete that had been spotless an hour ago.

"Of course you were laughing at me," Mary Beth continued, fuming. She'd halted Dan right next to the pile of dirty blankets. "Besides—"

"Mary Beth!" Lauren gasped. "Look what happened!"

"What are you talking about?" Mary Beth asked. Then she saw the mess and her jaw dropped. "W-what happened?" she stammered.

Lauren shook her head, and her lower lip began to quiver. "It looks like someone wrecked the barn—and it's almost time for inspection!"

7

"Who would wreck the barn?" Mary Beth asked.

Lauren turned slowly in a circle, surveying the damage. Things had been trashed, all right, but since nothing was ruined, she figured it was someone's idea of a prank. A lousy, mean prank.

"Maybe one of the other schools did it," she guessed, "one of our rivals." She looked directly at Mary Beth, then glared down the aisle toward Oldfields's section of the barn.

Mary Beth inhaled sharply. "Do you think *they* did this?"

A loud *thud* from one of the spare stalls made them both jump.

Mary Beth grabbed her arm. "What was that?"

"I don't know," Lauren whispered.

"Do you think it's the creeps who did this?" Mary Beth hissed.

Lauren nodded. Putting a finger to her lips, she tiptoed down the aisle. Mary Beth was right behind her. Looking bored, Dan took up the rear.

Halfway down the aisle, the girls heard a clunk. Lauren froze in her tracks. Mary Beth plowed into her, stepping on her heels. Dan stopped beside the two girls. Ears pricked, he gazed curiously toward the spare stall. The door was wide open.

"Even Dan's suspicious," Lauren whispered.

Raising his big head, Dan gave a low whinny. An answering nicker came from the stall. Lauren looked questioningly at Mary Beth. Her roommate seemed just as puzzled.

Just then, a fuzzy gray head peeked around the doorway. It was Applejacks!

The pony greeted Dan with another nicker. Strands of hay hung from his mouth.

"Applejacks!" Mary Beth exclaimed. "What's *he* doing loose?"

"Who knows? Come here, you stinker." Lauren took hold of the pony's halter and led him from the stall. "What are you doing in there?"

She peered inside the stall. Applejacks had knocked over every bucket and pulled mouthfuls of hay from every bale. Luckily, the grain bin was secured tightly.

Lauren shook her finger at him. "Look what you did!" she scolded.

"*He's* the prankster?" Mary Beth asked.

"It looks like it," Lauren said. "I wonder how he got out of his stall."

"Do you think someone let him out on purpose?"

Lauren shook her head. She didn't want to believe that anyone at the show would have done something that risky just to beat Foxhall Academy.

"Hey, how come the barn's such a mess?" Andie's voice demanded loudly from the other direction.

Lauren turned around. Andie and Jina were walking down the aisle. Andie's expression was stormy. Jina was glancing around, her brows scrunched in a worried frown.

"What'd you guys do? Set off a bomb?" Andie huffed. "The judges are going to be here any minute to inspect this place."

Mary Beth put her hands on her hips. "For your information, Perez, *we* did not make this rotten mess. It was *Applejacks*!"

"Applejacks!" Jina exclaimed. She stopped in front of the gray pony, a look of horror crossing her face. Applejacks pushed her arm with his nose.

"How did he get out?" Andie asked.

"We don't know," Mary Beth said. She checked over her shoulder, then whispered, "Maybe someone from a rival team let him out."

"What!" Andie cried. Even Jina's dark brows shot up in surprise.

"We don't know that for sure," Lauren said hastily. Tugging on the halter, she led Applejacks back to his stall. Jina followed her, then stopped in front of the open door to check the latch.

"There's nothing wrong with it," Jina said, her tone puzzled. She looked at Lauren. "What do you think?"

"I think we'd better clean up this mess before inspection," Lauren said flatly. She turned Applejacks loose in the stall and shut the door, making sure it was secure.

"I'll check that the other doors are closed," Jina said, hurrying to the next stall.

Lauren nodded. "I'll start cleaning up."

She found the broom knocked over in the extra stall. Mary Beth walked past, leading Dan. "What is this, disaster number five?" Lauren heard her mutter.

She poked her head out of the stall and smiled cheerfully. "Everything will be all right, Mary Beth. You'll see."

Andie barreled past, the dirty blankets piled in her arms. "I'm stashing these in the minibus," she told Lauren.

"Good. Don't worry, we'll get this place clean before inspection," Lauren said confidently. But when her roommate was out of sight, her shoulders sagged.

She hoped she was right.

"Could have been better, girls," the judge said fifteen minutes later. He ripped a sheet of paper from his pad and handed it to Katherine.

Lauren stood behind the judge, and when he wasn't looking, she stuck out her tongue at his back. He was the same sourpuss who had given Superstar a lousy score.

As soon as he had left, the eight girls crowded around Katherine, trying to see the sheet.

"Give me some room," the instructor said,

making shooing motions, "and I'll read it to you."

Lauren stepped away. Across from her, Mary Beth slumped against a wall. In all the confusion, Lauren had never finished explaining to Mary Beth why she and Tommy had been laughing. Now she wondered if Mary Beth even wanted an explanation. She looked as if she didn't care about *anything*.

"We earned a total of seven points out of a possible ten," Katherine announced.

Everyone groaned.

Katherine sighed. "It could have been worse. He marked us down on neatness of aisle and feed room."

Andie, Lauren, and Jina glanced at one another. They had been hurrying to finish when the judge came into the barn—five minutes early.

"But he did give us a perfect score for condition of horses and tack." Katherine grinned.

Ginny groaned. "So for tomorrow's inspection, no one leaves a stall door open, right?" She looked meaningfully at Jina.

"Hey!" Andie protested. "Are you saying Jina left Apple's door open?"

Ginny crossed her arms in front of her chest. "No, I'm just saying we'd all better be more careful." She glared at Andie. Andie glared right back.

Lauren rubbed her temples. She was getting a headache. Maybe some lunch would help.

She started toward Mary Beth, but Mary Beth turned abruptly and called to Missy and Heidi, "Hey, can I eat lunch with you guys?"

Lauren halted. There was no use trying to talk to Mary Beth now. Her roommate was obviously avoiding her.

"So what's with Finney?" Andie asked. She and Jina came up beside Lauren just as Mary Beth waltzed down the aisle with Missy and Heidi. "It seems like she's mad at us."

Lauren sighed. "She not mad at you guys. Just me."

"What'd you do?" Andie asked.

"She saw me and Tommy together," Lauren replied.

Jina frowned. "So? Why would that make her mad?"

"Ooo, I bet old Mary Beth's *jealous*," Andie snickered.

Lauren threw her hands in the air. "But there's no reason to be! I was just telling Tommy that Mary Beth was so freaked out before her class that she put the saddle on backward. We started laughing and Mary Beth saw us."

Andie snorted. "Finney put the saddle on backward? What a dope."

Jina folded her arms across her chest. "What is it about girls?" she said, sounding disgusted. "Once they get a boyfriend, they're never the same."

"Not me," Andie said. "I'm always the same sweet person."

Jina and Lauren exchanged glances. "Sure," Jina said. She squeezed Lauren's wrist. "Forget about Mary Beth. You have bigger worries right now—like acing your dressage test this afternoon. Foxhall needs the points."

Lauren grimaced. She didn't need to be reminded.

"Yeah. It wouldn't hurt to study a little before this afternoon's general knowledge quiz, either, Remick," Andie said. "We don't need you giving your usual boneheaded answers."

Lauren flushed. "Right." Turning sharply,

she tried to hide her pink cheeks from her roommates.

As usual, Andie's comment hurt. But Andie and Jina were right. She needed to forget about Mary Beth and concentrate on the show.

Concentrate on *jumping*, Lauren corrected herself. Because her team was counting on her.

"Okay, Lauren," Tommy called. "Approach the crossbar at a trot and use a mane release."

Lauren nodded. She was trotting Whisper in a small circle at the far end of the huge arena in Winter Oaks's coliseum.

At first the small chestnut mare had startled at every strange sight and sound. But after ten minutes, she was trotting smoothly in the tanbark.

"You do know what a mane release is, right?" Tommy's question echoed through the dome-roofed building.

Yes, I know what a mane release is, Lauren thought. It was a fancy way of saying "grab the mane so you don't pop your horse in the mouth when you jump." She also knew what a crest release was, and a short release and an automatic release.

She just didn't want to use them.

As Lauren circled Whisper, her heart began to pound and her palms started to sweat. That always happened when she even thought about jumping.

She peeked up at the stands, hoping no one was sitting there watching her. She didn't want anyone to know what a scaredy cat she was.

"Hey, Lauren, are you going to circle forever?" Tommy asked. He was still dressed in his breeches and black boots. He'd taken off his helmet, though, and was running his fingers through his wavy brown hair.

"Um, no. It's just that—" Lauren hesitated. Should she tell Tommy about this summer?

"Stop Whisper a minute," Tommy said.

Lauren sat deep and halted Whisper. Tommy walked over and looked up at her, a quizzical expression in his green eyes.

"I'm assuming you've jumped before. Otherwise your instructor wouldn't have entered you in a jumping class, even a beginner class," he said. "Right?"

Lauren looked down at her hands. She was clutching the reins so tightly that her knuckles were white. Whisper shifted impatiently.

"Right," she said in a small voice.

"So why are you so nervous? Did you fall off or something?"

Lauren squeezed her eyes shut. Suddenly, big tears began to splash down her cheeks. Hastily, she wiped them away with the sleeve of her jacket.

She took a deep breath. "No. I didn't fall. But last summer, during the Foxhall summer clinic, one of the other riders did. She'd brought her own horse and he—he crashed right into the fence. They were jumping in another ring over high fences. The girl was okay, but her horse—"

Dropping her reins, Lauren hid her face in her hands. She couldn't believe she was sobbing hysterically in front of a boy.

But she couldn't help it.

"What happened to the horse, Lauren?" Tommy asked gently.

Lauren bit her lip—hard. "The horse fell and didn't get up," she choked out. "They made all of us go back to the dorms, so I didn't see what happened. But I know what happened. That horse never got up again!"

For a moment, Tommy didn't say anything. Lauren swiped at her eyes. There, she'd said it. She'd told someone why she was so afraid of jumping.

But from Tommy's reaction, Lauren figured he thought she was foolish. After all, it wasn't as if she'd been in an accident herself. She hadn't even known the girl or her horse.

"Wow," Tommy said finally, looking up at Lauren. "That must have been awful."

Lauren sniffed. "Are you just saying that to make me feel better?"

He shook his head. "No way. You know what? The same kind of thing happened to me. I went to a steeplechase with my dad and one of the horses fell on the course. The veterinarian—" His voice cracked. "Well, I won't tell you what happened. But believe me, I still have nightmares about it."

Feeling relieved, Lauren slumped in the saddle. Tommy didn't think she was dumb. And somehow, telling someone what had happened made the whole thing seem a little less horrible.

"So. How can we make you not be scared anymore?" Tommy looked serious.

"It's not your job to get me over the jumping jitters," Lauren told him. "Unless you have some magic potion to make me suddenly brave—like you are over those big jumps."

Tommy shrugged and scraped his boot toe in the tanbark. "Nope. No magic. Just lots of schooling on different horses with my dad hollering at me."

"You could holler at me," Lauren offered.

He laughed. "Okay. Here's the plan. You said Whisper is a good jumper, and the fences in the beginner class are low. All you really have to do is aim her toward them, keep your leg on her so she doesn't decide to run out, and grab the mane. Simple enough?"

Lauren nodded. "Aim, use leg, grab. I can remember that."

"Maybe once you go over the first fence,

you'll forget about the, uh, accident."

"I hope you're right. Well, here goes." Lauren squeezed her heels against Whisper's sides. The mare moved off eagerly. Her ears flicked back toward Lauren, waiting for the next cue.

At least Whisper's ready, Lauren thought as they trotted toward the practice jump.

"Good approach," Tommy called.

Suddenly, the image of the horse crashing into the wall of poles flickered through Lauren's mind. She tried to blot it out with a picture of Jina and Superstar flying over a fence.

Then she saw the rest of the picture. The two of them had landed so hard that Superstar bowed a tendon!

The painful memory of Jina's last show made Lauren's stomach churn. She stiffened the same moment Whisper took off.

Grab mane! she told herself frantically. Reaching high on Whisper's neck, Lauren closed her fingers around two braids. The mare rounded her back, then straightened her forelegs. She landed safely and cantered easily toward the end of the ring.

Lauren felt like cheering. *We did it!*

She circled Whisper, and they trotted back

to Tommy. When they halted, Lauren threw her arms around the mare's neck.

"I should have trusted Whisper," Lauren said. "She was perfect."

"Smooth as silk," Tommy said. He had a funny look on his face.

Lauren giggled. "You don't need to say it. I know I stunk."

"Well, I wasn't going to use that exact word," Tommy said with a laugh.

Lauren had to laugh, too. Then Tommy checked his watch. "Do you want to try one more? I have five minutes left before I have to get ready for my next class."

"I guess I'd better." Lauren shortened her reins. As she turned Whisper toward the other side of the arena, she saw a girl who'd been sitting in the stands jump quickly to her feet.

Lauren immediately knew who it was.

"Mary Beth!" she called. But her roommate was running up the steps. Taking the steps in twos, Mary Beth leaped to the concourse at the top of the stands.

"Hey! Mary Beth!" Tommy waved to her, but she'd already disappeared.

"Oh, great," Lauren muttered.

"What was that all about?" Tommy asked,

frowning. "Why'd she run off like that?"

Lauren didn't know what to say. She certainly couldn't tell Tommy that Mary Beth was acting like a jealous jerk.

Besides, she didn't have time to discuss Mary Beth's love life. Tommy had another class and she had to study for the general knowledge quiz before her dressage test. *And* she had to jump one more time. This time it was going to be perfect.

Half an hour later, Lauren and Jina were perched on hay bales in the spare stall, with sodas and bags of chips beside them. Jina was giving Lauren a pretend quiz.

Outside the stall door, Andie groomed Magic, who stood crosstied. Lauren hadn't seen Mary Beth since she'd disappeared from the coliseum.

"Name the five phases of the horse's jump," Jina read from the question sheet.

Lauren wrinkled her brow and tugged anxiously on her braid. *Jumping* again. It seemed like she couldn't get away from it.

Even though Tommy had helped her get over the practice fence a second time, she knew she'd looked terrible. There was no way she would get a ribbon, even in a beginner class. She just hoped her teammates wouldn't be too disappointed.

Lauren turned her attention back to the question. "*Five?* Are there really that many phases to the horse's jump?"

"Yes, there really are, bonehead," Andie hollered from the aisle.

Jina nodded in agreement. Sometimes, Lauren wished her roommates weren't quite so intent on helping her. It just made her feel dumber.

"Do I have to say them in order?" she asked, still stalling.

"Yes," Jina said impatiently. "If you don't know the answer, just say so."

"I don't know it," Lauren blurted. She grinned sheepishly. "But I did get the first three questions right."

"That's true," Jina said. "But this one is worth five points. If you get it wrong, it'll really knock down your score."

Lauren made a face. "Rats," she said.

Just then Mary Beth strolled into the spare stall. She glanced at Jina and Lauren, then looked quickly away.

Lauren's stomach twisted in a knot. She

didn't know what to say to make her friend feel better.

"Hi," Jina said.

"Hi," Mary Beth muttered. "I'm just in here to get my bridle. I need to clean it."

"Did you finally find the right bridle for Dan?" Lauren asked, her voice cracking.

Mary Beth just nodded as she sorted through the tack hanging on the portable rack.

Jina gave Lauren a questioning look. Lauren shrugged and took a gulp of soda.

"So what's wrong with you, Finney?" Andie asked loudly from the doorway. She leaned one shoulder against the doorjamb. "Jealous because Lauren stole your wimpy boyfriend?"

Lauren nearly choked on her soda. "Andie!"

Mary Beth whirled around, her face beet red. "No, I'm not jealous," she retorted. "I couldn't care less about Tommy. Whoever gave you the idea that I was jealous?" She turned on Lauren, her eyes snapping. "Let me guess. I bet it was the same disloyal jerk who laughed at me while I was riding."

Mary Beth stuck her nose in Lauren's face. "And the same jerk who snuck off to the coliseum to be alone with my boyfriend!"

Lauren gasped and shrunk away from Mary Beth's accusing eyes. She'd had no idea her roommate was so furious.

Andie and Jina gazed at Lauren in surprise.

"You were with Tommy in the coliseum?" Andie asked.

"I, um, I—" Lauren stammered as she glanced back and forth at her roommates. They were all glaring at her as if she were some kind of criminal.

Just tell them the truth, a voice said inside Lauren. *Tell them he was helping you jump.*

But Lauren didn't feel like confiding in her roommates right now. She was sick of worrying about winning ribbons and getting right answers on the dumb test. And she was sick of Mary Beth's accusations.

Without a word, Lauren leaped to her feet, almost knocking Mary Beth over. Then, pushing roughly past Andie, she raced down the aisle.

She didn't know where she was going and she didn't care.

She just wanted to get away from the whole stupid show.

Lauren ran out of the barn and into the bright sunlight. Squinting, she looked around for someplace to escape to. Maybe she could hide in the minibus or hang out for an hour or two at the concession stand.

No, Lauren thought gloomily. *Those are dumb ideas.* Sooner or later, she was going to have to face her roommates and the other team members—and all the things that were bugging her.

I might as well do it sooner, she decided.

Squaring her shoulders, Lauren strode to the first ring, where Katherine was leaning on the top rail, sipping a soda. She was watching a Hunter Over Fences class.

"Hi, Katherine," Lauren said.

The riding instructor was watching a sleek

black horse leap over a gate decorated with plastic flowers. "Hello there," she said. "What's up?"

Lauren took a deep breath. "I'm sorry, but I'm *not* going in that jumping class. Foxhall will just have to lose the points."

Katherine raised one brow. "Oh? What made you change your mind?"

"I *never* wanted to go in it," Lauren declared. "I *hate* to jump. I only said I would because it seemed like I absolutely had to."

"Oh." Katherine shrugged as if it were no big deal. "Well, that's okay. This show is supposed to be fun, not torture. I'll wait until morning before I scratch you from the class, though. Okay?"

At first, Lauren stood frozen, afraid she hadn't heard right. Then it hit her: *she didn't have to jump!*

"Okay!" she said happily. Leaning on the fence next to Katherine, she waited for the rush of relief.

She waited and waited. But nothing happened. Instead, the feeling that she was letting Foxhall down slowly began to gnaw at her insides.

With a heavy sigh, Lauren propped her chin

in her hands and stared unseeingly at the horse in the ring. *What's the matter?* she wondered. *I should be so happy.*

Lauren's bottom lip quivered as she realized what the problem was. She was too disappointed in herself to be happy. She was going to let her team down.

"How's that?" Andie asked as she lowered Lauren's right stirrup an hour later.

Lauren stuck her boot toe in the iron. Whisper stood patiently while she flexed her ankle. "It's still too short."

Andie rolled her eyes in exasperation. "Why are your stirrups so short, anyway?" she asked as she dropped the buckle one more time.

"I was schooling Whisper over a jump."

"Oh, that's right. You *were* entered in Beginners over Fences." She smirked up at Lauren. "Too bad those big two-foot-high fences were too *scary* for you."

Oh, shut up, Lauren thought as she tested out the stirrups for the third time. She felt bad enough. The whole team was already talking about why she wasn't jumping.

Lauren pushed her weight in her heel. "That's better, I think." She rose in the saddle as if she were posting. She'd forgotten how hard it was to go from a short jumping position to the longer leg needed for dressage.

"So why are you so scared to jump?" Andie asked. "You've done it before."

Lauren let out her breath. "I don't want to talk about it."

"Then will you at least tell me if you and Finney ever made up?"

"No."

"Too bad. Jina and I thought she was nuts," Andie continued. "We told her you weren't interested in wimpy Tommy and that she was ruining a good friendship over a stupid boy."

"You guys really told her that?" Lauren asked in surprise.

"Sure." Andie grinned. "We still like you, even though Foxhall will lose mucho points since you're not jumping. Roomies need to stick together."

"Thanks—I guess."

Andie smoothed Whisper's quilted saddlepad. Then she glanced up at Lauren, her eyes twinkling. "We *did* wonder why you and Tommy were all alone in the coliseum."

Lauren giggled. "Believe me, it wasn't a date."

Andie tilted her head, waiting.

Lauren rolled her eyes. She knew Andie would never give up until she had an answer. "Oh, all right, if you have to know. He was helping me jump."

"That's it?" Andie frowned. "Why didn't you ask me to help you jump? Then Finney wouldn't have gotten all bent out of shape."

"I didn't want anyone on the team to know how scared I was," Lauren said in a small voice. "It seemed so stupid."

Andie shrugged. "Just medium stupid. So do you want me to tell Mary Beth what you two lovebirds were doing?"

"Yeah, thanks. Maybe she'll believe you." Lauren tightened the chin strap on her helmet. "I've got to warm up Whisper before the dressage test. You'll need to be at the arena at exactly three-twenty if you're going to be my reader."

"Yup." Andie pulled a copy of the training-level test from her pocket and held it up. "I'll be there. Good luck."

As Lauren rode Whisper to the warm-up area, she reviewed the sequence of movements in her head. In her last test, she'd had trouble remembering the order This time, Katherine had allowed a reader to help in case she got confused, but Lauren wanted to make sure she knew it by heart.

"Enter working trot, sitting," Lauren murmured to herself. "Halt. Salute. Proceed sitting trot. C—track right. No, *left*," she corrected quickly.

Lauren shook her head, trying to clear it. She could still see Mary Beth's accusing eyes. Would her roommate ever be her friend again?

Whisper walked and trotted smoothly around the warm-up area. Sitting deeper, Lauren increased her leg pressure and at the same time closed her hands to steady the reins. The mare responded by rounding her neck and body and moving energetically forward. Lauren grinned. She loved it when Whisper felt powerful, yet balanced.

"It's three-fifteen, Remick!" Andie waved from the side of the warm-up area.

Lauren's heart flip-flopped. *I'm not nervous,* she told herself. *I can do this.*

She had to.

Whisper broke into a jig as they strode toward the dressage arena. It was a rectangular area flanked by white posts marked with black letters. At one end, the judge and the scribe, a volunteer who wrote down the judge's comments, sat behind a desk that had been set inside the back of a horse trailer.

Lauren took a deep breath, trying to calm herself down. She didn't need Whisper catching her butterflies.

She stopped next to the ring steward, who was holding a clipboard in her hand, waiting for the rider before Lauren to finish.

"You're on," the ring steward told Lauren when the rider gave her final salute. Lauren urged Whisper forward. They trotted counterclockwise around the outside of the arena, passing in front of the judge's trailer.

Out of the corner of her eye, she glimpsed Andie, walking toward *E*. Her roommate gave her the thumbs-up sign.

Lauren smiled. It made her feel better that Andie was there. And she really was glad that Andie and Jina believed that she wasn't after Tommy. After all, he was just a friend. A cute, really nice guy who had tried to help her with a tough situation.

Then a horrible thought made Lauren swallow hard. *What if she really did like Tommy?*

The sudden ring of a bell made Lauren jump in the saddle. *Pay attention,* she told herself. *That's your cue to enter the arena!*

Lauren trotted Whisper down the side and into the arena. Tommy's smile flickered before her face. *No way*, Lauren thought, squeezing her eyes shut tight. *There's no way I like Tommy as a boyfriend.*

"Halt. Salute!" Andie called anxiously from the sidelines.

Lauren's eyes flew open. She caught her breath as her mind suddenly focused on the fact that she was in a dressage arena riding a horse in front of a judge.

Abruptly, Lauren pulled Whisper to a halt. The mare stopped square.

"Thanks, Whisper," Lauren murmured. She dropped her right hand to her side at the same moment she nodded in a salute to the judge.

To do well in dressage, she and Whisper had to be completely in sync with each other. She couldn't daydream or worry about her problems.

Concentrate, Lauren told herself fiercely. When the judge saluted back, she picked up the rein with her right hand and signaled Whisper to trot. Then she pushed all thoughts of Tommy and Mary Beth from her mind.

10

"I can't believe it!" Andie exclaimed when she came running up to Lauren after the test. "You almost blew it!"

Lauren halted Whisper. "It's just like math," she said with a sigh. "I have trouble concentrating during a test."

She dismounted, landing on the ground with a thud, and hugged Whisper's warm neck. "Thanks, girl. I couldn't have done it without you."

"That's for sure," Andie grumbled. Since a sharp wind was blowing, she'd brought Whisper's cooler from the barn.

"You were supposed to go in there and win for Foxhall," Andie said as she threw the cooler over Whisper's back. Angrily, she jerked it up the mare's neck, flopping it against Lauren's helmet. "Instead you almost forgot to salute!"

"Oh, shut up, Andie," Lauren said. "It's just a stupid show." Turning abruptly, she loosened Whisper's girth a hole and ran up the stirrups.

Andie silently tugged and yanked the cooler. Then she let out an exaggerated sigh. "You're right. Sorry I yelled. It's just that Foxhall's had such lousy luck so far. And actually, once you remembered to halt, the rest of your test wasn't bad."

"Really?" Lauren asked.

Andie nodded. "Whisper performed like a pro. I watched a couple of other horses before you. They were pretty bad."

"Maybe I have a chance, then," Lauren said hopefully. "But I won't know until I see my score."

She glanced toward the judge's table. Usually, a runner took the scores to the secretary to be computed, then posted. "I'll probably have to wait an hour or so."

"Let's hope you get a first or second," Andie said as they started walking back to barn A. "Jina and Applejacks got a fifth in their hack class. And Mary Beth had that beginner's skills class. I think everyone won a ribbon unless they fell off. And Ginny and Alicia both had decent rides in their dressage tests."

"Great. Maybe Foxhall will actually end up with some points before the day's over," Lauren said, wishing it *was* over. "I can't wait to get to the hotel. Did you know they have an indoor pool?"

"Yeah, but don't forget—we all have to take the general knowledge test before we can have any fun."

Ugh. Lauren stopped in her tracks. She *had* forgotten about the test.

"Come on. Let's get Whisper back to the barn," Andie said. "After she's untacked and cooled off, we can check your score. Foxhall could use some good news."

An hour later, Lauren, Andie, and Jina stood in front of the bulletin board outside the secretary's office. Several other kids were clustered around it. Lauren didn't recognize any faces, but one boy wore Manchester school colors.

"Have they posted the team standings yet?" Jina asked as she scanned the board.

Andie shook her head. "No, they're going to make us wait until tomorrow morning. But

Katherine's been nosing around. So far, Foxhall's in the bottom third."

Lauren wrinkled her nose. "That doesn't sound so hot."

"Hey, Lauren," Jina said, pointing to one of the sheets. "There are the scores from your dressage test."

Lauren's gaze ran down the list, noticing that not all the scores had been filled in yet. When she came to her number, her heart pounded excitedly. She'd gotten a 56.5 percent!

"Jina! Andie!" She grabbed her roommates' arms. "So far, I've got the highest score! Maybe Foxhall has a chance yet!"

"Ah, a bed!" Jina declared as she fell backward on the queen-sized mattress.

"Ah, a real toilet!" Andie cried. She hurried into the adjoining bathroom, dragging her bulging backpack with her.

Lauren dropped her overnight bag and flopped on the other bed. Her stomach was growling, and she could still taste the garlic from the pizza they'd wolfed down before coming to the hotel.

Mary Beth stood by the door, clutching the handle of her suitcase with both hands. As she gazed around the room, she shifted awkwardly from foot to foot.

"What's wrong?" Lauren asked her.

"I was just trying to figure out who was going to sleep with who—whom, whatever." Mary Beth nodded toward the beds.

Jina struggled up on her elbows. Her eyes were bloodshot and a piece of hay was stuck in her ponytail. "I'm so tired, I don't care who I share with."

"That's the truth." Lauren yawned. "All that work for a fourth place. I think I'll go to sleep right now."

She closed her eyes. Instantly, her brain filled with questions from the knowledge test. *Where's the stifle? How many beats in the canter? How do you tell a horse's age?*

Groaning, Lauren opened her eyes again. Each school team had gone to the coliseum to take the test. Everybody had spread out in the stands. Lauren had fretted over each question. She had no idea how well she'd done, but she was sure glad it was over.

She was glad the whole day was over.

Just then, the bathroom door swung open. "Last one in the pool is a rotten egg!" Andie sang out.

"What?" Lauren lifted her head. Arms out-stretched, Andie struck a pose at the foot of her bed. She had changed into a neon-blue tank suit.

"Are you crazy?" Jina asked. "It's too late to swim."

Andie crossed her eyes and wagged her tongue. "Of course I'm crazy."

"I'm going swimming, too," Mary Beth announced. Dropping her suitcase on the floor, she opened it and pulled out her suit. "Tommy's meeting me."

"So that's why you want to go swimming," Jina said to Andie. "*Boys.*"

Andie pretended to look hurt. "Of course that's not the reason." Grabbing Lauren's arm, she pulled her to a sitting position. "Come on, Remick. Wake up. It's time for a little fun."

Lauren sagged like a rag doll. She looked over her shoulder at Jina. "What do you think?"

Jina grinned. "I guess we'd better go and keep an eye on these two. Otherwise, they'll probably get themselves into some kind of trouble."

Fifteen minutes later, all the girls were in their bathing suits. Lauren slipped on flip-flops and a pink T-shirt.

When they stepped out into the hall, Lauren knocked on the door next to their room. Katherine opened it a crack and peered out sleepily.

"We're going swimming," Lauren told her.

Katherine nodded. "Dorothy's already down there. Don't swim too long. We're all getting up at six sharp, so set your alarm. I'll be knocking at your door at seven. Inspection's at eight-thirty and this time we have to be ready."

"Aye, aye, Captain!" Andie saluted. Lauren, Jina, and Mary Beth giggled. Katherine just rolled her eyes and shut the door.

"Dorothy's back?" Jina asked as they hurried to the elevator.

"She must be," Lauren answered. "I wonder how the Foxhall riders did at that other show."

Andie snorted. "Better than us, I'm sure." She stopped in front of the elevator and pressed the button for the lower level. A minute later, the doors opened. The elevator was packed with kids wearing bathing suits.

"I'll wait." Lauren stepped back quickly. Most of the kids had competed at the show. She didn't feel like listening to their comments.

"I'll wait, too," Mary Beth said.

Jina and Andie pushed into the elevator. Andie waved as the doors closed.

Lauren waited for a minute, then pressed the button again. Mary Beth stood silently beside her.

Lauren stared down at her hands. She wondered if Mary Beth would ever say anything. *Should I say something?*

"Mary Beth, I'm—"

"Lauren, I'm—"

Lauren giggled anxiously. "Sorry. You go first."

"No, you go first," Mary Beth insisted. Her freckled cheeks had flushed pink.

Lauren clutched her towel tightly. "I wanted to say I'm sorry you thought Tommy and I were doing something behind your back. I mean, we *weren't*. I like Tommy. But just as a friend."

"I know." Mary Beth shuffled a bare foot along the carpet. "The show was just so nerve-wracking. Nothing seemed to go right. I guess I took it out on you. I'm sorry."

Lauren nodded and they both smiled shyly.

"Friends?" Lauren asked.

Mary Beth grinned. "Friends." Then her grin faded. "But you know what really bugs me?"

Oh no, Lauren groaned silently. *What now?*

"Andie in a bathing suit," Mary Beth went on. "Did you see her? I mean, she has a *figure.*"

"I know," Lauren said. "Jina, too. It's not fair." She glanced at her own flat chest, then at Mary Beth's. Over her bathing suit, her friend wore a baggy T-shirt that hung to her knees.

"I think I'll leave my T-shirt on while I swim," Mary Beth said solemnly.

"Me too," Lauren said. "Do you think anyone will notice?"

"Let's hope not," Mary Beth said, and they both giggled loudly.

The doors opened. This time no one was in the elevator. Still giggling, Mary Beth and Lauren hung onto each other as they stumbled inside.

When Lauren stepped out at the lower level, she heard laugher and shouts from down the hall. She and Mary Beth followed a trail of wet footprints to the heart-shaped pool. It was surrounded by potted palms, and a fake waterfall spilled into one end. Several kids stood on a ledge, diving into the cascade of water.

On the other side of the pool, Dorothy was sitting on a lounge chair, sipping a soda and talking to Alicia and Missy. The barn manager still wore jeans and a sweatshirt, but Alicia and Missy had changed into skimpy two-piece bathing suits.

"Don't look now, but more curves to our left," Lauren whispered, and Mary Beth snorted with laughter. Lauren was glad they were friends again.

"Let's put our towels over by Dorothy and the others," she suggested.

"Good idea. Do you see Andie or Jina anywhere?" Mary Beth asked as they walked around the crowded pool.

Lauren shook her head.

"How about Tommy?"

"No. Don't worry, we'll find them."

Just then, Lauren heard a bossy voice shouting across the pool. It sounded like Andie.

It *was* Andie. In the middle of the pool, she was standing nose to nose with a girl from another school.

"You and your stupid friends are losers!" Andie hollered. Her wet hair clung to her shoulders and her eyes snapped angrily. "Foxhall may not be first today, but we will be tomorrow!"

"No way," the other girl scoffed. Her auburn hair was dry and hung in a perfect bob. "Foxhall will be dead last."

"Wanna bet we win?" Andie challenged.

"Yeah, I'll bet." Smirking, the girl glanced over her shoulder at some kids, then she turned back to Andie. "If Foxhall doesn't win, your team has to clean all our stalls."

Lauren gasped. There was no way Foxhall could win that bet. Not in a million years.

"Fine," Andie said confidently. "In fact, if Foxhall doesn't win, we'll clean *all* the stalls at Winter Oaks!"

11

"Did you hear what Andie just said to that girl?" Mary Beth exclaimed.

Lauren nodded in disbelief. Andie's big mouth often got her in trouble, but it was hard to believe even she had made such a stupid bet. Foxhall couldn't possibly win.

"I'm telling Dorothy, " Mary Beth declared. "Maybe she can make Andie apologize and take it back."

"Wait!" Lauren grabbed her roommate's elbow, jerking Mary Beth backward. Her friend slipped on the wet tiles and fell on her butt.

"Are you all right?" Lauren bent to help her up.

"Hi. Are you guys having fun?"

Lauren glanced up. Tommy was standing

beside her. Water ran off his narrow chest and dripped from his baggy suit onto his bony white legs. His brown hair was plastered to his head.

Lauren looked down at Mary Beth and they both burst out laughing. Obviously, they weren't the only ones who didn't have perfect bodies.

"Oh, we're having a great time," Mary Beth said as she struggled to her feet. "Especially since tomorrow we'll be mucking out the stalls until midnight."

"Huh?" Tommy looked puzzled.

"Didn't you hear the bet Andie just made with that girl?" Lauren pointed to the auburn-haired girl. She was leaning back against the edge of the pool, her hair still perfectly dry.

"Andie made a bet with Jennifer Schwartz? Why?"

"Because Andie's a dope, that's why," Mary Beth muttered.

"Jennifer's from Westminster," Tommy told them. "Their team's in first place."

Mary Beth and Lauren moaned in unison.

"And, boy, do they let everyone know they're the best," Tommy added. "They're a bunch of snobs."

"That's probably why Andie got so mad." Lauren tapped her lip with one finger. "I think this calls for drastic action."

Mary Beth raised one brow. "Oh? Like what?"

"Like maybe a super-cannonball to show Jennifer Schwartz that the Foxhall girls mean business."

"Ohhh." Mary Beth nodded knowingly.

Lauren kicked off her flip-flops and threw her towel on an empty chair.

"A super-cannonball?" Tommy repeated.

Lauren nodded. "Yup." She and Mary Beth began sauntering toward Jennifer.

"Hey, I'm in on this, too," Tommy called, hurrying to catch up. The three of them halted at the edge of the pool right beside Jennifer and her friends.

"Jump on the count of three," Lauren whispered.

She waited until the area was clear, then hollered, "One, two—*three!*"

Leaping high into the air, she wrapped her arms around her knees and landed with a loud *thwap* in the pool. Tommy and Mary Beth landed on either side of her. Water exploded in the air like an erupting volcano.

Blowing bubbles of laughter, Lauren swam to the surface. Jennifer stood a few feet away, staring at her in horror. The girl's hair hung down her face like soggy seaweed.

"What did you do that for, you creeps?" she sputtered.

"Because we're *Foxhall* creeps," Lauren shot back. Just then Mary Beth surfaced, and Andie and Jina swam up, laughing. The four girls put their hands together and chanted, "Foxhall, Foxhall, we can do it all!"

Lauren stretched and yawned. The hotel room was dark and everyone was still fast asleep. Turning on her side, she checked the red numbers on the digital clock.

7:00 A.M. Yawning again, Lauren rolled on her back, careful not to bump Jina who was curled beside her. Then she sat bolt upright.

7:00!

Whipping back the blanket, Lauren leaped from the bed and sprinted to the window. She yanked back the heavy curtain. Sun streamed into the room.

Lauren screamed.

"What? What?" Mary Beth jerked up to a sitting position. "Is it on fire?"

Jina groaned and hid her eyes. Andie pulled the covers over her head. "Close those curtains!"

"We're late!" Lauren screamed. Rushing across the carpet, she started to pull clothes from her overnight bag. "We were supposed to get a six A.M. wake-up call. And it's seven now! Katherine and Dorothy will be knocking any—"

Two sharp raps on the door made everyone gasp.

"Are you guys ready?" Dorothy called.

Horrified, Lauren looked at her roommates. They stared back, looking just as frantic.

"In a minute!" Andie called finally as she, Mary Beth, and Jina scrambled out of bed. "We'll meet you in the coffee shop!"

Jina disappeared into the bathroom. Mary Beth was right behind her.

"What happened, Remick? Did you forget to phone the front desk about that wake-up call?" Andie snapped. She was tugging a comb through her tangles and pulling on her riding shirt at the same time.

Wiggling and twisting, Lauren pulled on clean breeches. "No, I didn't forget. I called them and told them six o'clock!"

"I heard her do it," Mary Beth mumbled from the bathroom, a toothbrush stuck in her mouth.

"Well, *somebody* messed up," Andie accused.

Grabbing her dirty pajamas, Lauren threw them in her suitcase. "Quit worrying about it and get ready," she told Andie. "We have five minutes to get washed, dressed, and packed."

And we'll never make it, she added to herself.

"Ugh. I never should have eaten those pancakes so fast," Mary Beth moaned forty minutes later as the minibus bumped down the drive toward Winter Oaks. She and Lauren sat in the backseat.

Lauren nodded. "I know what you mean." She'd only had cereal and toast, and her stomach was churning.

Dorothy peered at them in the rearview mirror. "Well, if you girls had gotten up earlier, you could have had a nice leisurely breakfast like the rest of us. Now we're going to be late getting to the barn. Luckily, the others left forty-five minutes ago."

"We would have, too," Andie grumbled. She was huddled in the front seat between Dorothy and Jina. "If Lauren hadn't messed up."

"She did not mess up," Mary Beth defended Lauren.

Andie snapped her head around. "Oh yeah? Then who did?"

"Girls!" Dorothy barked. "Quit arguing and start thinking about what you need to do when we reach the barn. Katherine will have fed the horses, but the rest is up to the team."

"She's right," Mary Beth said. "Today we have to get one hundred percent on our inspection and win every blue ribbon. Otherwise we'll have to *muck out all those stalls.*" Leaning forward, she shouted the last sentence in Andie's ear.

Andie didn't even turn around. "Oh, shut up, Finney."

As the minibus pulled up to the barn, Lauren quickly reviewed in her head what she needed to do. First on the list was helping Andie and Mary Beth get their horses ready for their class, Walk Trot. She knew Andie was nervous because she was riding Magic for the first time in a show.

And Mary Beth was always nervous when she rode.

Lauren sighed. At least it would be an easy day for her. Since she'd decided not to jump, she and Whisper were entered in a Hunter Under Saddle class, where they would just have to walk, trot, and canter.

It would be a piece of cake.

When the minibus halted, everyone piled out and ran into the barn. Alicia, Ginny, Heidi, and Missy greeted them with razzes and boos. Lauren wondered if they knew about Andie's bet.

"It's about time you lazy bums got here," Heidi called. She was sweeping the aisle.

Missy gave them a raspberry. "At least this time none of your horses got loose and trashed the place."

Flushing, Lauren ducked into the spare stall. She couldn't blame the other team members for being mad at them.

"Well, I know what I have to do," Andie said, following her. "Longe Magic or he'll explode when I get on him."

Lauren hunted for Dan's grooming kit. "I'll brush Dan," she told Mary Beth. Her roommate was standing in the doorway as if she had no idea where to start. "Maybe you should wipe off your bridle and boots."

Nodding woodenly, Mary Beth went over to the bucket of tack-cleaning supplies. Jina grabbed Applejacks's halter and headed out the door with Lauren right on her heels.

The two girls were rushing down the aisle when Lauren saw Jennifer Schwartz turn the corner and head toward them. Two of her friends were walking beside her. All three girls were dressed in their show outfits, looking perfect.

"Well, hello, *Foxhall* girls," Jennifer said with fake sweetness. "Hurrying to get ready?"

"That's right," Jina said. "There's lots to do."

Arching one brow, Jennifer smiled. "Too bad you got here so late this morning." She turned to her friends. "Right?"

They snickered and nodded.

Slowly, Lauren set the grooming kit on the ground. "How did you know we were late?" she asked, clenching her fists by her sides.

"Easy. We were the ones who let you snooze a little longer."

Lauren gasped. "You guys canceled our wake-up call?" she asked in disbelief.

"Did I say that?" Jennifer pretended to look puzzled. "Did I say anything about a wake-up call?"

"I bet you did it," Lauren said. She narrowed her eyes. "Did you also mess up the barn and let Applejacks out?" she asked, about to lose her temper.

Jennifer gasped in mock horror. "Us? Now why would we do a thing like that?"

Scowling angrily, Lauren took a step forward. If she'd been Andie, she would have punched Jennifer Schwartz right on her perky nose.

"Temper, temper," Jennifer said, wagging a finger in Lauren's face. "It's your own fault you're late. Besides, it doesn't matter how early you got here or how clean your stalls are—your team still won't win."

Turning, Jennifer wiggled her fingers at Lauren and Jina. "See you later, Foxhall. And don't forget to bring your pitchforks."

"Boy, would I like to rub manure in their faces," Lauren steamed after the older girls had left.

"Save your energy for the show." Jina shook her head. "I can't believe they'd do something as low as cancel our wake-up call."

"Me neither. They must have been *really* mad we got them all wet." Lauren giggled, then picked up Dan's grooming kit with a sigh. "At least everyone will know for sure it wasn't my fault. Not that it makes any difference.

Jennifer's right. We won't win that bet, no matter what."

Jina shrugged. "We might have a chance. If we get ten points for inspection and all of us win a first, second, or third in our classes —"

"Including the jumping class," Lauren said under her breath.

Jina's brows shot up in surprise. "You're going to jump Whisper after all?"

Lauren nodded. "I have to. It would be stupid to give away those points." She stood a little taller. "I'm going to try my hardest to win a ribbon," she said. "Because there's nothing I'd like better than watching snotty Jennifer Schwartz muck out Whisper's stall!"

12

"Would you guys relax?" Lauren said to Andie and Mary Beth. Her roommates were mounted on their horses, waiting by the in gate. Using a clean towel, Lauren wiped some dust from Andie's boot.

"I *can't* relax," Mary Beth complained. "It's bad enough riding in this stupid class, but now, because of Andie's dumb bet, I have to win a first or second."

Andie rolled her eyes. "Oh, grow up, Finney," she snapped. Nervously, Magic swung in a circle, almost knocking Lauren over. "*That's* no big deal. Dorothy told me Mrs. Caufield is coming this morning, and I know she's going to watch me like a hawk. I've got to convince her I can handle Mr. Magic. *That's* a reason to be worried."

You're both wrong, Lauren thought gloomily as she gave one last swipe to Andie's boot. *Jumping over fences is a reason to be worried.*

"Are the children fighting again?" Jina teased as she came up with a can of hoof polish.

Lauren forced a laugh. "Yes. Let's send them to their rooms," she joked, but inside her stomach was twisted in knots. She wished she could take her own advice and relax.

"Come on, Mary Beth. Lauren's right," Andie said. "We need to pull together and win first and second in this class. Heidi and Windsor can win third. That'll show those Westminster braggarts we're a threat."

"Ha!" Mary Beth said. "That may sound like a piece of cake to you, Andie. But winning a ribbon isn't so easy for me." Craning her neck, she scanned the spectators. "Has anyone seen Tommy this morning? He said he was going to watch my class."

"Who'd want to watch a bunch of dopes like us?" Andie asked.

"Tommy, that's who," Mary Beth said huffily.

"All riders for Walk Trot please enter the ring," the announcer said over the loudspeaker.

Mary Beth jumped in her saddle. "That's me—us!" she squeaked.

Lauren gave the calf of her boot a reassuring squeeze. "You can do it. Just quit worrying. And good luck, Andie."

"I'll need it." Andie glanced over her shoulder toward barn A. "Tell me if Caufield shows up in time to watch the class," she called as Magic pranced toward the in gate. Dan plodded after him.

Jina sighed. "I think Andie will need all the luck she can get," she said, moving to the rail for a better view.

Lauren watched the handsome Thoroughbred dance into the middle of the ring. Andie patted his neck soothingly, then turned him in a small circle.

"I think they'll both need it," Lauren said. Her gaze went to Mary Beth and Dan. Mary Beth's head kept bobbing around as she hunted for Tommy.

Jina glanced sideways at Lauren. "What did Katherine say when you told her you were going to jump after all?"

Lauren's stomach lurched at the mention of the "j" word. "Not much. She's going to help me warm up Whisper after your Pony Hunter

Under Saddle class is over. Are you ready?" she asked anxiously. "You might be the only one who can win a blue for Foxhall."

Jina nodded. "Apple and I should do well unless something crazy happens."

"Jina! Jina! Jina!" a shrill little voice rang across the show grounds. Lauren and Jina turned to see a girl about seven years old jogging toward them, leading a pony. Her curly blond hair bounced as she tugged the balky pony closer.

"Oh, no," Jina said under her breath. "It's Whitney. And she's got Applejacks." She shot Lauren a pained look. "Did I mention the word 'crazy'?"

Lauren bit back a giggle. Whitney Chambers was Applejacks's official owner. But since she was so young and just learning to ride, Jina had been schooling the pony for her.

"Did Apple win any ribbons? Did you jump? Do you have another class? Can I ride him?" Whitney asked excitedly as she yanked the gray pony toward them. When she reached Jina, she squealed and wrapped her arms tightly around Jina's waist. "Oh, I'm so happy to see you!"

Jina ruffled the little girl's unruly hair. "Hi,

Whitney." Even though Whitney could be a brat sometimes, Lauren knew how much Jina liked her.

"I'm glad you came," Jina said, plucking the lead strap from Whitney's grasp. "But you shouldn't have taken Applejacks from his stall."

Whitney stuck out her lower lip. "He's my pony, and I can do whatever I want with him."

"Yes, but at a show, he's my responsibility," Jina said firmly. "Okay?"

Ignoring Jina, Whitney jumped up on the lowest rail of the fence, then leaned over the top rail into the show ring. "Hey, there's Andie and Mary Beth. Hi, Andie and Mary Beth!" she shouted, waving furiously.

Jina rolled her eyes. Wrapping her arms around Whitney's waist, she pried her off the railing and set her on the ground. "Whitney, you can't yell like that."

Whitney started hopping up and down. "Can I ride now? Can I? Can I?"

"Whitney-y-y." Jina let out her breath in exasperation, and Lauren choked down a laugh.

"Applejacks has a class in about half an hour," Jina explained. "I was just about to tack him up. So listen, Whitney, I . . ."

Instantly, Whitney's lower lip stuck out even farther. "But you said . . ."

"Hey, I know what!" Lauren bent to Whitney's level. "Why don't you ride him back to the barn bareback, like the Native Americans used to?"

"Bareback?" Whitney's whole face lit up. "Cool!" She turned to Jina. "Can I?"

"That's a great idea," Jina said. "Quick thinking," she whispered to Lauren.

"I used to baby-sit," Lauren whispered back. She stepped closer to Whitney. "Here, I'll give you a leg up."

She boosted Whitney onto Applejacks's back and showed her how to twine her fingers in his mane.

Instantly, the little girl started to pump her body and pound her heels against the pony's sides. "Let's gallop!"

"Oh, no," Lauren frowned with mock seriousness. "The Native Americans only walked their ponies. Unless, of course, they were chasing buffalo."

"Oh, right." Whitney nodded, just as serious.

Jina threw Lauren a grateful smile, then led Whitney off. With a relieved sigh, Lauren turned back to the ring. The twelve riders were lined up in the middle. Dan stood like a statue. Beside him Magic bobbed his head and pawed the ground impatiently.

Lauren was glad to see that Andie was keeping her cool. She calmly moved Magic forward, circled him behind the other riders, then halted him at the other end of the line.

"Here are the results of class twenty-four, Walk Trot," the announcer called. "First place goes to Speedo, owned by Westminster Academy and ridden by Miriam Rosenthal."

Westminster! Lauren's heart sank. That would make the bet even harder to win.

"Second place goes to Dangerous Dan, owned by Foxhall Academy and ridden by Mary Beth Finney."

"Yay, Mary Beth!" Lauren cheered loudly, raising one fist in the air. She'd done it! Her roommate had won a red ribbon.

Lauren darted around to the exit gate. Mary Beth and Dan were just walking from the ring. Mary Beth's face was frozen in a smile of disbelief.

"Did you hear that, Lauren?" she gasped. "Dan and I won another ribbon. A *red* one!"

Lauren nodded enthusiastically. "You did great!"

Mary Beth dismounted just as Tommy came up. He was wearing jeans and a hooded Manchester sweatshirt.

"Congratulations," he told Mary Beth. "You and Dan were awesome."

"Awesome?" Mary Beth hooted. She gave Dan a hug. "Let's just say we did okay."

Standing on tiptoes, Lauren craned her neck, trying to see if Andie or Heidi had won a ribbon. Heidi rode Windsor from the ring, a yellow ribbon for third place fluttering from his browband. Moments later, Andie and Magic left with the six girls who hadn't been pinned.

Andie halted Magic away from the others. Lauren pressed her lips together. She knew how hard Andie had been working with the big horse. She hoped her roommate wasn't too disappointed.

"I'm going over to Andie," Lauren told Tommy and Mary Beth.

"Hi. You did good," Lauren said when she reached her. Andie was facing the saddle, running up a stirrup.

"Yeah, Magic did do well," Andie said. "I

was really proud of him. Only I don't think Caufield will see it that way."

"She's here?"

Andie nodded. "She was standing on the other side of the ring." She lifted the saddle flap to loosen the girth, and the big horse pranced playfully away from her.

"Whoa. Stand," she said firmly.

"Andie!" someone called.

Lauren and Andie turned at the same time. The Foxhall riding director was striding toward them.

"Congratulations." Mrs. Caufield beamed. She was an attractive woman in her early forties. Her graying hair was pulled back by a barrette, and she wore a long quilted coat over jeans and paddock boots.

Andie looked at her in surprise. "For what? We didn't win anything."

"For doing a super job with Magic," the director said. "You kept your head and your cool. Winning a ribbon on Magic will come much later."

Relief flooded across Andie's face and she broke into a huge smile. Lauren felt tears come to her own eyes. Quickly, she wiped them away, feeling a little foolish.

Maybe Foxhall wasn't going to win the most points at the show, but things had turned out great for two of her roommates. Mary Beth had won a fifth and a second. And Andie and Magic had come through their first show with flying colors.

Now it's my turn, Lauren thought.

A sudden sharp stab of fear made her clutch her stomach, and bile rose in her throat. She'd been so concerned about her roommates that she'd forgotten about her upcoming jumping class.

Turning away from Andie and Mrs. Caufield, Lauren pressed her fingers against her eyes. Immediately, she pictured a horse, its eyes white with fear, crashing headfirst into a wall of poles.

But this time, she knew the horse.

It was Whisper.

That afternoon, Lauren waited nervously out-side the in gate, mounted on Whisper. Her roommates were clustered around her.

"When you approach the first jump, take a deep breath every third stride," Jina told her.

"No, no." Andie shook her head vehe-mently. "That's all wrong. When she approaches the jump, she shouldn't think about breathing. She should be keeping Whisper steady and—"

"Hey!" Mary Beth interrupted, shouting above the others. "I don't know anything about jumping, but I do know lots about being afraid. I think she should picture something nice in her mind, like a—"

Dropping her reins, Lauren put two fingers in her mouth and whistled shrilly.

Startled into silence, her three roommates looked up at her.

Lauren held up her hands. "Thanks, but that's enough advice," she said quietly, picking up her reins again. "Whisper and I will figure this out for ourselves."

Jina nodded and started to push Andie and Mary Beth away. "She's right. Let's leave her alone."

"Leave her alone?" Mary Beth protested. "But who's going to—"

"Enough, Mary Beth," Jina hissed, giving her an extra-hard nudge. Mary Beth stumbled into Andie.

"Hey, you klutz," Andie protested as the three of them walked off. "Just because you won *two* ribbons . . ."

Lauren had to chuckle. Her roommates meant well, but they were driving her crazy. She hadn't told them how she'd imagined Whisper crashing into the fence. And she wasn't going to. They had already given her tons of confusing advice.

While she waited to be called, Lauren rode Whisper around the other entrants, trying to calm her racing heart. She didn't recognize any of the other riders, but she knew they were all beginning jumpers, too. They were probably just as scared as she was. Maybe *more* scared.

But Lauren knew she had one big advantage: none of them had a horse as special as Whisper. Even though Lauren had been tense and anxious during warm-up, the small mare had done her best.

"You really are the greatest," Lauren said, patting Whisper's neck. "I'm so glad Mrs. Caufield assigned you to me that first day."

Suddenly it dawned on Lauren why she needed to conquer her jumping jitters. Not to win ribbons or bets.

But because she loved Whisper.

She, the rider, was like a pilot. And it was up to her to guide Whisper safely over the jumps.

Fifteen minutes later, Lauren was trotting Whisper toward a small gate, the first jump in the last line of fences.

"Just two more," Lauren murmured to Whisper. "Two more and we're done."

Whisper flicked one ear back, listening. Trying to follow all of her roommates' advice, Lauren took a deep breath, steadied her reins, thought about chocolate milkshakes, and—

Whisper sailed over the jump. She was so

smooth, Lauren wasn't even aware of reaching up the mare's neck in an easy crest release. She didn't notice the mare's hooves hitting the ground when she landed. And she didn't realize that they'd cantered to the next jump and flown effortlessly over it.

All Lauren knew was that they'd finished and Whisper hadn't crashed. Her heart was pounding so loudly, she couldn't hear the cheers of her hysterically happy roommates.

"How many stalls have we done?" Mary Beth asked as she glanced down the empty aisle. It was getting late, and Westminster's horses and riders were long gone. "I don't want Dorothy to leave us."

"We've got two more to do," Lauren said, pitching a forkful of straw into the wheelbarrow. Flipping the pitchfork over, she raked together the last bits of dirt, manure, and straw.

Mary Beth held her nose. "This stuff stinks. Didn't those prissy Westminster girls ever clean their horses' stalls?"

"If they did, they didn't do a very good job." Lauren threw the last forkful in the wheelbarrow, then pushed the barrow past Mary Beth and into the aisle. Jina and Andie were working in the next stall.

Lauren poked her head inside. Andie was leaning tiredly on her pitchfork handle, watching Jina rake.

"So what do you guys think?" Lauren asked. "Did those lazy Westminster snobs pile more straw on top of the old instead of cleaning their stalls?"

Jina nodded. "Definitely. There's no way they should have earned a ten on their barn inspection. Too bad it's too late to rat on them."

"Yeah. Then Foxhall would have won instead of Westminster," Mary Beth declared.

Lauren looked at Jina, then Andie. The three of them burst out laughing.

"What's so funny?" Mary Beth asked.

"Mary Beth, there's no way Foxhall could have won," Lauren explained. "We weren't even close."

Mary Beth's face fell. "Oh. Well, then it's a good thing Westminster didn't hold us to Andie's bet to clean *all* the stalls at Winter Oaks." She glared at Andie. "Or we'd be here until tomorrow." Leaning against the doorjamb,

Mary Beth sighed dramatically. "It seems like this whole show was a lot of work for nothing."

"What do you mean, nothing?" Andie protested. "You won two ribbons."

"And you got to see Tommy," Lauren added.

Mary Beth flushed. "True."

Jina stopped raking. "I think we all got a lot out of the weekend. At least I did. It was fun taking Superstar to a show again. And two ribbons proved Applejacks and I could get along."

"Yeah. I guess I proved something, too," Andie said, straightening up. "I showed everyone I could stay cool enough to handle Magic. He's definitely the horse for me." She tapped her lip. "I just have to figure out a way to buy him. . . ." Her voice trailed off as she stared into space.

Lauren hid a grin behind her hand. She had no doubt that her roommate was cooking up some wild scheme to convince her dad to buy Magic.

"And let's not forget *you*, Lauren Remick." Jina pointed her rake handle at Lauren. "You proved you could jump."

Lauren looked down at the toes of her sneakers. "It was still pretty scary."

"But you did it," Mary Beth said, clapping her on the shoulder.

Lauren smiled slowly. "Yeah. I did, didn't I? Still—" she started pushing the wheelbarrow to the next stall "—you have to admit, this was the craziest horse show ever."

"Maybe," Jina said as she and Mary Beth followed her, "but I think we did okay."

"Not just okay," Andie said, hurrying after them. "We did great, roomies. I think we deserve a cheer."

The four girls formed a circle, their right hands in the middle. Lauren grinned happily at her friends.

It *had* been a great show.

Then she joined Andie, Mary Beth, and Jina as they raised their clasped hands in the air and shouted, "Foxhall, Foxhall, we did it all!"

**Don't miss the next book
in the Riding Academy series:
#9: ANDIE'S RISKY BUSINESS**

Mary Beth giggled. "So, what are you going to do? Steal Magic?"

"Hey, good idea, Finney," Andie said with a scowl. "I could hide him in the bathroom."

"Hide a thousand-pound horse in the bathroom! Are you kidding?" Mary Beth exclaimed.

Andie pressed her lips together. "Of course I'm kidding." She sat up and swung her legs off the bed. "If I steal Magic, I'll have to take him to another barn."

Jina furrowed her dark brows. "Andie, you wouldn't," she warned in that same superior tone Andie's father always used.

Andie sighed and slumped backward. Of course she wouldn't steal Magic.

Unless she was desperate.

**If you love horses, you'll enjoy
these other books from Bullseye:**

THE BLACK STALLION
THE BLACK STALLION RETURNS
THE BLACK STALLION AND THE GIRL
SON OF THE BLACK STALLION
A SUMMER OF HORSES
WHINNY OF THE WILD HORSES

ALISON HART has been horse-crazy since she was five years old. Her first pony was a pinto named Ted.

"I rode Ted bareback because we didn't have a saddle small enough," she says.

Now Ms. Hart lives and writes in Mt. Sidney, Virginia, with her husband, two kids, two dogs, one cat, her horse, April, and another pinto pony named Marble. A former teacher, she spends much of her time visiting schools to talk to her many Riding Academy fans. And you guessed it—she's still horse-crazy!